…YOUR PLACE
OR
MINE?

By the Same Author

To Whom It May Concern

...YOUR PLACE OR MINE?

Shariq Iqbal

Srishti
PUBLISHERS & DISTRIBUTORS

Srishti Publishers & Distributors
N-16, C. R. Park
New Delhi 110 019
editorial@srishtipublishers.com

First published by
Srishti Publishers & Distributors in 2013

All characters in this book are fictitous, and any resemblance to real persons, living or dead, is coincidental.

Typeset by EGP at Srishti

Printed and bound in India

ACKNOWLEDGEMENTS

Thank you, Ammi and Abbu, for being the best parents ever. Clichéd but true.

Saima, for being such an exacting critic, good you're my sister otherwise I'd have gone bankrupt paying you.

Faiza, for being my little sister, and for being the brightest thing in my life.

Srishti Publishers' entire team, for making me feel like an author.

God, for looking after me in more ways than I could have asked for.

And finally, you, for picking up this book.

"There's a story behind everything, but behind all your stories is always your mother's story. Because hers is where yours begin" —Mitch Albom

Dedicated to my Ammi, for bringing out the best in me.

"All the truth in the world adds up to one big lie"

—Bob Dylan

PROLOGUE

"You bastard! What is wrong with you? Get the fuck out of here!" her voice droned out into the loud music as I moved away, ducking at just the right moment as her glass came flying at me. The bouncer came and stood next to me and the music suddenly stopped with sharp sound of glass shattering on the floor.

"Sir, you better leave right away or we'll have to escort you out," he whispered into my ear.

"Alright, I'm outta here" I announced with my hands raised and smiled at all the faces staring at me.

Stepping backwards, I had one last good look at her, her black tube-top and heavy makeup shone sharply in the dimly lit pub, with her widened eyes fixed at me and her shriek still haunting the air around, she had probably pulled off a perfect break up scene. One which would definitely make me look like dumped, and would fodder her mind into drinking all night, with complements like 'you gave it to that loser' and 'that dick sure deserved it' acting as add-ons.

Stepping out in the open, into the cold night and away from the jarring music, I let some peace seep into my head and felt the moist breeze hit my face. Glancing around to make sure there were no cops checking drunken driving, I got into my car, lit a cigarette and sped away with a screech.

After driving for a while, when I was almost about to reach my apartment, I diverted my car and took the usual turn towards the long elevated highway, to burn rubber and probably looking for a vent to burn away the bitterness of the night.

Though I had lost count of the number of times I had sped hard on this straight stretch of asphalt with the darkness of the night and thick Marlboro smoke surrounding me, the moment never failed to pull me in the introspection mode that I always come here for.

My name is Ali, and right now, sucking hard on this cigarette and feeling life at hundred kilometres per hour, I get a short lived feeling that I'm awesome.

Once this car comes to a halt and the cigarettes in this pack are over, what remains is my uninviting bed and a dreamless, dead sleep into a dull morning, where the only person who truly loves me impatiently waits to catch a glimpse of me to hand me over his token of love, which comes in form of long computer codes and project deadlines.

There was one more love though, four years back, which came in a relatively more attractive and preferable form, her name was Divya, when people saw us together, right from early college days, they said we would get married and it would be the most perfect love story that they would ever see.

Last year, we got married, she to 'a well settled guy in the States' and I to this pack of Marlboros. "Shit happens dude, relax," this is what they had to say.

As I press harder on the gas pedal, I see an infinitely dotted, smog engulfed Bangalore skyline. I pull over to the side of the lane and step out in the numbing yet comforting silence of the night.

Probing into the dashboard a little leads me to an old marijuana joint which I could really use right now. As I light it and take in the smoke a couple of times, the smell after a long time draws me into deeper, more awful introspection.

My name is Ali, and whenever I begin to think anything about my life apart from the next day's project or the coming deadline, all I can think of is a woman called Divya.

Till a year back, I didn't had to smoke marijuana leaning on the parapet of a flyover at three o clock in the night to think about her, but shit happens, as they said, and I'm doing so now.

With the fast diminishing joint clipped between my fingers, I loosen the knot of my tie and run my palm over my hard, thorny stubble, and suddenly realise that I'm not awesome. I'm miserable, wretched and weak.

I drive a sedan and have a fat wallet, but when I look at the setting sun from the balcony of my twentieth floor apartment, I get a jolt of realisation that I'm down and out.

Taking long, dark puffs of the burning grass makes my eyes teary, or maybe it's because of the view of the long, palely lit stretch of road running under the flyover.

At a distance far ahead, I notice two youngsters riding an old, creaking motorcycle. Through the smoke and tears blurring my vision, I can decipher that they are hooting randomly and their bike knows no direction.

One of them stands behind the rider and unbuttons his shirt, raising the bottle in his hand and yelling a triumphant cheer to the sky.

The other one responds to him by a similar shriek rattling into the silent night.

They look aimless, purposeless and broke, but they are awesome.

The guy riding the bike suddenly looks straight at me, his hazy face gradually becoming clear and the smoke around me giving way for his piercing, almost mocking smile.

I try to smile back but a closer look at his face throws an unsettling, disturbing reality at me.

I know the guy. His name is Ali. And his shirtless friend in the pillion is Sandy, and I was right, they are aimless, purposeless and broke, but they sure are awesome.

1

OF MARIJUANA AND MEMORIES

"Woohoooo" Sandy suddenly stood up making me lose control of the bike for a moment.

Clenching hard on my shoulder and raising the bottle in his hand up in the air, he tried to balance himself and sang in a hoarse, intoxicated voice, *"Moon river, wider than a mile... I'm crossin' you in style... I'm crossin' you with smile..."*

"Get down! The bike will crash!" I looked at him only to find him shirtless and facing the sky. "Put on your shirt back! There can be cops on next turn! Are you listening to me?" I shouted at him trying to surpass the bike's screeching drone.

"Fuck you, fuck you, fuck you!" that was all he responded with for the rest of the ride until we reached the hostel.

Yeah, we're guys, drinking and abusing is how we make merry.

I rode the bike shakily through the drizzly, cold night, strongly reeking of marijuana and with my vision blurring repeatedly.

The guard manning the entrance ceased to matter to the final year seniors. Though there were more important things that mattered now, fourth and final year in an engineering college meant placements. And with the season about to kick off from the next morning, the corridors were abuzz with activity when we reached the hostel past midnight.

Happy Singh came rushing towards me as I reached my room ready to crash into my bed, "*Oye*, placements tomorrow..." he said thumping me hard on my back.

"So?" I asked drowsily, "Everyone knows that."

"But still dude. Imagine! Placements! Jobs!" he said grinning at me from ear to ear and left.

If I'd shown even half his enthusiasm, he'd have surely given me one of his *Punjabi* bear hugs, one that's famous in the hostel for introducing you to the real scent of a man, and no, it's not what those deodorant ads claim it to be.

I looked at the long corridor before going into my room, all the rooms had their lights on. There were guys moving around with neatly ironed shirts and some of them introduced themselves to the air.

I wondered what the coming days held for me. "Hey, which company is coming tomorrow?" I asked Murthy as he went past me in one of his hysterical walks up and down the corridor.

"Dude, not now please. I'm in no mood for fun" he said and others standing aside laughed at him.

They thought I was trying to make fun of the way this nine-pointer-scholar was going all frenzied the night before the placements started.

I laughed back trying to make it look funny. To me, it wasn't. I really didn't know the name of the company.

✿✿

"Why are your eyes red?" that was the first thing the sharp looking, gray haired interviewer asked me as I went and sat across him in the interview room.

I was wearing one of the shirts Happy had ironed and abandoned at night realizing that the colour or the checks didn't suit the momentous occasion he was about to witness.

With a bitter mouth and a throbbing head, I forcibly sat upright in front of the interviewer and answered, "Sir, this company holds a lot of value for the students in the campus. The reason my eyes seem red is, since yesterday night I have been continuously researching the kind of questions you can ask me and the kind of mindset I have to carry in this room to prove my abilities and to make a lasting impression on you. But right now, feeling your suave, gentlemanly aura and the way you represent this organization, I think I came very ill-prepared and still need to go back and spend more nights to touch the bar that you've set. I hope I'm wrong here but I'm also afraid to admit that my reasoning tells me that I'm right."

He looked at me trying to sync in my heavily loaded answer, "I never said you aren't good. Tell me more about yourself." He said looking into the resume that I'd printed after replacing Happy's name with mine.

"Sir, I'm a person who believes in hard work and dedication clubbed with constant desire to excel" realizing this was going a little mundane, I added, "and it will be just gibberish if I say that money doesn't motivate me or it isn't a driving factor for me, it sure is, and I don't take any shame or pride in admitting so. It's just that I like taking up responsibilities, and I hold hard work in high regard"

I was doing just as Divya had advised me to, my lines were coming out exactly as I'd mugged, for a moment I let my dope parched attention wander and the interviewer sitting in front of me suddenly dissolved into Divya, "Preppy! You're doing good! Those words, god! They're heavy. Where did you learn to talk like that? Who's the wise man who taught you this? Or wise-woman I should say!"

Suddenly the reality pitched in, in form of gray hair and hoarse voice, and a series of questions, which I tackled with similar jargon and self degrading words, came my way. "They want to feel superior. They want to see you degrade yourself and praise them for no specific reason. If you don't find anything to appreciate in them, they'd surely have bald patches and ugly, grumpy faces, so congratulate them for achieving that in life," Divya had told me one afternoon a few days before campus interviews started.

Soon I was done with the long and tiring interview, walking under the hot afternoon sun along the long and dusty path leading to the hostel, I wondered how I'd done.

Interviews mattered to each and every student on campus, except for this half naked creature I found lying dead on the bed as I entered the room.

"Wake up asshole. We'd interviews today" I said kicking Sandy.

"*You* had interview... Not *we*" he said yawning, "and wait, did you really go and attend that interview?" he said and sat up straight on the bed.

"Yes isn't that obvious?"

"Obvious my ass! Didn't I tell you that my dad will get both of us a job? I've told him already... He knows half the companies in Bangalore" he said and shut the bathroom door behind him.

"Maybe, but not this one. This is EnY. You should've atleast attended this one"

"EnY? What does that stand for?" he shouted from inside.

"E*nst and Young! You seriously didn't know that?"

"You seriously expected me to know that?" he replied.

I set out on my bike to ride through the long road connecting my campus and NIMS Medical College.

Around three years back, on the same spot that I'm passing through right now, I'd met Divya.

I remember how I stuttered and stammered and how her every word ringed in my ears when I went back to the hostel that night.

And I remember going through sleepless nights and numerous daydreams and how she got etched into my mind and into my life eventually.

It's funny when we recollect, especially when there are no regrets, or when we don't pay heed to regrets and just recall and smile.

So I lit a cigarette, slowed down my bike and recalled and smiled.

It's also funny how sometimes all you want from yourself is to stop recalling the same thing that once made you smile.

It happens, everyone has a story and I too have one, right in this city and not outstretching outside the confines of these roads and these few friends that I have, we all have one, and mine like many others around me, is one of regrets and solace, of cold comfort and hard reality, of love and despair, and of fragile happiness and lasting helplessness.

That day when I reached NIMS college hostel, where Divya used to stay, I never knew I'd return with that lasting helplessness stuck onto me like a leech.

"Preppy, my course is coming to an end so dad's calling me to the US. He wants me to stay there for a month and do my intern in a hospital there," I remember her saying.

That night, we went out like always and returned to NIMS campus late into the night.

"I'd be leaving tomorrow" she said as we reached near ladies hostel.

"What?"

"I thought I wouldn't tell it to you straight away in the evening and spoil your mood."

"Spoil my mood? As if this helps. How can you leave tomorrow?"

"I have to preppy. You know how my dad is, he's sending a car at six, so I don't think I'd even sleep now. It's one already"

"Sending a car? Can't I just drop you at the airport?"

"Not possible. The car will be coming for sure and it'd be better if the driver doesn't see me with you. You just wait for me here, it's just one month preppy"

Just one month. I thought to myself. It was unnerving.

It was almost five when I started my bike and decided to leave; her image soon disappeared in the foggy dark night as I rode the bike out of the campus.

We'd it all figured out, finding a job was important to me right now as I had to get to her dad with a job in hand and ask him to let Divya marry me.

This was our plan, it was plain and simple - we love each other, so let us marry.

I entered the room and switched on the light.

The poster just above Sandy's bed had a jubilant Muhammad Ali standing tall over a badly knocked out opponent with the words *"I'll hit you so hard, all your plans will fail - Muhammad Ali"* written at the bottom, this is what he had told that opponent in a face-off before the match.

Over the old poster Sandy had scribbled in his own handwriting, *"'I'll hit you so hard, all your plans will fail' – Life"*. I ignored that.

"Today a new company is coming. Try to get up and come to college. Atleast attend this one" I told Sandy while putting on a set of neatly ironed formals. Four years of college were soon coming to an end within a few days, everybody had atleast something to talk about interviews except Sandy, he still hadn't attended a single one of them yet, and I knew he wouldn't attend any now.

My chances of landing a decent job seemed far from possible, I either went stoned in front of the interviewer or wanted to be with Divya to feel sane.

I'd last heard her voice that day in NIMS campus, after that we'd either just chatted online or had gone days without even that.

She'd written one long mail explaining how stringent her

parents were and how badly she was stuck in the rigorous hospital job and her dad's incessant remarks about her lifestyle.

Everything in my life was making it important for me to get a job, and right now, as I take my seat in front of this interviewer, his forced smile and 'I-know-you-are-good-for-nothing' expression right away tells me that this one too is gone.

"Hi, what's your name?" he grunted while going through my resume which had my name in big bold letters on top of it.

"And Ali, tell me why I should take you?" he continued without waiting for my answer.

"Sir, I'm hardworking, diligent and I know how to work under deadlines. I don't balk seeing challenging work and I want to learn more and more and increase my abilities"

"Everyone sitting outside has exactly the same qualities as you just mentioned. Strange isn't it?" he said smirking at me, "I'll give you one more chance, tell me what's so special about you so that I've no other choice but to take you"

"Nothing" I said in a bland tone.

"What? Did you just say?"

"Nothing" I said it again.

I knew this was crazy but I really had nothing special to talk about me.

I was a twenty two years old engineering student. I'd just made it to the passing grades most of the times and had scraped through many of my subjects in second attempts, there was little blood and flesh left in my marijuana system, and only thing I learnt in my four year stint at this college is how to write long paragraphs full of nothing in exams and how to be a recluse.

Only bright aspect of my life was sitting miles away right

now and the face of this interviewer didn't go very well along with all that.

"So, that means we are done" he interrupted my train of thoughts and handed me my resume.

I got up and left.

The setup of plastic chairs and rickety wooden tables at Manju bhai's *dhaba*, a local eatery behind college, was the most relaxing ambience I'd found till now.

I knew I'd just screwed up a job interview and the placement's calendar in college had no more companies coming for now, but all my mind was able to think was about Divya.

I wanted to talk to her, wanted to tell her that I'd foiled our plan by not getting a job and by acting like a jerk in the interviews.

All this I couldn't talk on chat, and Sandy didn't care to know, I'd nobody to confide to and felt like a loser, which was an obvious realization that just struck a little late.

I entered the room to find loud music with heavy haze of marijuana smoke.

Sandy, Happy and a few others were passing each other a fat, smouldering joint. Like always, nobody acknowledged my entry and without even taking off formals, I took a deep dark drag of the grass.

"I'm coming from an interview" I said looking at them.

"Shhh, smoke up and shut up" Sandy said and others huffed out a laugh.

Happy's heavy pat landed on my back, "Tell her, she listens to all our pains, and gives the answer too" he said signalling at the joint.

As usual, I smoked up heavily and woke up late into the night.

I could remember that the high I got was full of Divya, and though I was too reluctant to accept it, that signified that even marijuana was not helping now.

"Preppy, I've a surprise for you." Sandy said as I sat on my bed recovering from the deep sleep.

"Shut up asshole. I'm hungry" I murmured.

"I know. So let's go out and celebrate my surprise preppy" he said clapping mockingly.

"Fuck off. Can't you be serious sometimes?"

"No. Now get up and come"

"Where?" I asked puzzled.

"To eat and yes, to celebrate my surprise" he again said with a wide grin.

It was one in the night and we sat at an all night open Coffee Day which was brimmed with loud people.

"What's your surprise?" I asked eating my third brownie.

"Preppy, we need to talk. I think I want to break up" he said smirking and kept his hands on mine.

"Fuck you idiot... Stop calling me that! And do you have something even remotely sensible to talk?" I said going back to my brownie.

"I'm serious. I mean not the preppy part, but yes, we're breaking up." He said again smirking.

"Sandy, please. What is it?" I asked irritated.

"Tomorrow, I leave for Goa. Dad's opened a new factory and I think he's in serious mood to go bankrupt by asking me to handle it. So technically, we're breaking up right? Right preppy?"

"What? Goa? You serious?" I asked in shock.

"My sense of humour is random I know. But not as random

as to make this up out of nowhere. We have to part preppy, God what will I do without you"

"Shut up idiot. I can't believe this. You are going all the way to Goa. What's happening man!" I said thumping the table.

"College's over remember? And easy, this isn't even the surprise" he said and got up picking up the bike keys.

"What? So what is that now?"

"Nothing" he said and grinned at me. The word suddenly reminded me of morning's interview.

Sandy left at four in the evening the next day.

There wasn't any send off as he hadn't told anyone.

We just smoked a joint and tried to relive the innumerable good old times through that.

It was strange, I wasn't upset about it, but seeing off Sandy gave me a jolt of reality, college had come to an end and so was hostel.

I felt all by myself as one of Sandy's gleaming chauffer driven car came to pick him up.

"Don't say a word" he said hugging me and hopped in his car.

I stood there amid a dust cloud, seeing his car and the past four years coming to an end just like that.

After an hour I got a message from Sandy, "Get out of your bed and go out you dope-head!"

I read the message and walked out of my room. As soon I reached the corridor Happy Singh pounced towards me and hugged me so tight that I thought I'd pass out.

Everyone in the gallery looked at me and smiled.

"What's happening?" I asked pushing Happy away.

"EnY's final list is out."

"So?"

"Ass you really don't know that your name is there in that?" Happy came close to me and asked in a serious tone.

"What? My name? In EnY?" I murmured looking around.

Suddenly my phone beeped, 'Now that's called a surprise motherfucker' - It was Sandy.

When I walked out of the hostel for the last time, carrying my heavy steel trunk that I've been checking in and checking out into various hostels since past eight years of my life, it was hard for me to digest that this too, like other hostels, was coming to an end.

I saw people around me who were yet to get a job, if they'd befriended Sandy, probably all they'd to do was tell him the name of the company.

Sandy's favour was a huge one, I tried to thank him over the phone but he always had too much to tell me about his life in Goa and how his several managers handled everything and all he did was smoked hash and transformed into an Indian hippie.

He was yet to understand how huge his steel factory was but had figured out a corner to grow marijuana and was already in talks with the gardener there.

I remembered cursing him for not understanding my anguish of not getting a job and how the only thing he ever asked me about placements was the full form of EnY, when there was avid placement's talk in every room of the hostel.

Sandy left me with a void by not discussing how and what he'd done after asking me just the name of the company that day.

Getting a job at EnY was a glamorous thing on campus as

it was one of the best on offer, the lecturers who abhorred me came forward to bid me goodbye and wished me luck.

My hostel mates knew about my lifestyle so they were yet to figure out how EnY did such a screw up.

Nobody even in their wildest dreams knew what had actually happened, and that included me.

I told Divya I'd landed a job and that too the best one on campus.

I typed several times that it was all actually because of Sandy but deleted it every time.

I finally just told her that my start date was just two weeks away, after her extended internship she should be coming back to India in another month at maximum, and pleaded her to find time to call me from a public phone.

Things did seem brighter for a change even though I'd no one to talk to in Bangalore, the thought of asking Divya's dad to let her marry me after a few years kept on hovering in my head.

Sandy always said that it was a huge 'man thing' to do and that'd be one part of his life where he'd try to be serious, if at all he'd not decide to spend his life with Goan hippies, and he wouldn't contemplate that until he gets to see his will.

I boarded a train to Delhi to go home and meet my parents.

With a pack of cigarettes and few of hostel friends, I sat in the sleeper class bogie of a weary Indian train and relived the old times.

EnY's huge office and Divya awaited me back here after a couple of weeks, with similar thoughts and many little kids as my co passengers, I smiled into the open sky and thanked God for the long forgotten little peace of mind that I experienced after several months.

sure I was f[illegible] good here and I was to directly report to

2

I'LL DO IT ALL

"This is Michael. And he's the *Mai-ka-lal* here" this is how I was introduced to Michael.

EnY had an enormous office in the commercial hub of Bangalore.

After my three day initial induction, I was told to report to Michael, a fat and fair American whom the company must be paying in sacks to leave his country and stay here.

Only person I'd befriended till now was a guy much older than me, Raja, he roamed around in khaki uniform and his job was fixing computers and allotting people their desks.

Raja had a typical rash Hindi dialect which would get showered with expletives once he stepped out of the office.

When he first told me that 'Mai-ka-lal' told him to make sure I was finding it good here and I was to directly report to him, I didn't understand what was happening.

That day when he directed me to Michael's cabin and I entered and met him for the first time, the meeting left me shocked, and in a way, humiliated.

Michael was the head of India operations which meant nobody sat over him in India.

When all new recruits were assigned to various projects, I was asked to directly work under Michael as a part of the project team he was heading.

That unwillingly led me to conclude that Sandy's dad would've phoned Michael and had asked him a favour, to take me in and baby sit me under him.

"You must be.. aaa.. Alley.." he said in a heavy American accent as I entered his cabin.

"Yes, yes sir. Ali" I said looking at his round and Barbie pink face which seemed to have a smile permanently stuck over it.

"Nobody is called 'sir' here. Call me Mike in front of me and fat bastard behind me like others do. That will suffice." he said as I looked at him in shock.

"Don't worry mate, here the rule is, work your butts off. If calling me fat bastard helps, call me that all day." he said permanently smiling and controlling his accent understanding I'd met him newly.

A middle aged serious looking man entered the room, "Alley, meet Nagesh, he's your team lead."

I shook hands with him.

"Nagesh, show him around, he's new here" Michael said and turned towards his monitor.

Nagesh showed me my desk and immediately handed over a heavy pile of documents to me, "Go through them all, these are confidential so you can't take them home. Start reading and let me know when you're done" he said and left without waiting for me to ask or say anything.

Sometimes, out of nowhere you strangely want to hug your mother to get over all the coldness around you. I looked around; I wish I could do just that.

Days passed and I fell into a monotonous routine of work and home, I rented an apartment on twentieth floor of a high rise near office.

It had two big rooms and a large, awkwardly empty hall. I set up all the stuff I'd gotten from hostel in one of the rooms and spread my mattress on the floor there, which eventually became the only area I used in the house.

I used to call Sandy and persuade him to come and work in his dad's Bangalore unit, but like always, he'd too much to talk about Goa, from his making out sessions on the beach to his villa where he stayed alone in company of his six dogs.

Every weekend I called him hoping to find him in the same dull and boring state like me but the loud music and voices on the other side of the phone always made me hang up saying I'll call later.

Strangely, I cut down on my cigarettes and marijuana became a college memory, last joint being the one I'd smoked with Sandy the day he left.

My room was the same mess like it used to be in hostel, just minus one bed and an addition of a wardrobe full of formals. I'd asked the maid to never bother about that room and she rarely had anything to clean up in the remaining unused house.

My bank account brimmed with monthly paycheques. I never felt the urge to splurge on anything; I had no one to talk to and nothing to spend money on. I spent the weekdays at office and weekends curled up in my bed, sometimes sleeping for forty hours straight.

In office I left my desk only for food and smoke, my primary work used to be coordinating with people sitting in UK and doing some tweaking and updating in the code.

Michael used to chat with me occasionally; he was from California where he had a divorced wife and their three kids.

Divya rarely called but mailed almost everyday, saying she'd be coming in a month and that was the only thought influencing above all the thoughts in my head, be it at office or at home.

Her every expression, everything she used to talk used to remain in my head for days, I saw her in dreams, got up thinking about her and went home tired in the evening with her in my mind.

✿✿

That morning when I reached office, as usual I kept my bag on my desk, switched on my system and went out to the open area where Raja would be hanging around waiting for me.

After smoking a cigarette with him, I came back to my desk and checked my mail. I'd been waiting for a mail from Divya since a week now and saw one today, expecting it to be a long one, I opened it and started reading.

"Ali, I'd been trying to tell you this since long. Take care of yourself."

Under the text, I saw an attachment of a picture file.

I opened it and saw Divya cosily hugging a guy whom I don't recognize. They both are smiling wide into the lens. It's a self-portrait. There's a ruffled bed in the background.

Bombs exploded. I looked around, it was all calm. No one heard them except me.

There was a ringing in my head. I quietly got up from my chair, ignoring the voices and faces around and I straightaway headed towards the open area.

There, I lit a cigarette and just stood numb and looked into the open sky.

That evening, I worked till midnight, and wished there was more work.

I took the stairs down as the silence in the elevator would force me to think about what was happening. I sat in my cab and asked the driver to take me to some place where I can get good weed at this time.

I got up in middle of the night with my office wear still on, I realised I'd smoked up badly after coming home.

I went out to the balcony looking for fresh air.

Staring into the dark and cold night from my twentieth floor apartment, I began to cry.

I clenched my face and wept hard, only holding myself from wailing loudly.

There was too much to think and too much to understand from what I'd seen in that mail today.

Divya had left, and she did so through that one email.

I quietly got up and went back to my room without looking across the empty house.

There was more stuff in the packet and I made one more, larger joint out of it.

I smoked up hard until I passed out to sleep.

✿✿

"Alley, you look messed up, everything fine?" Michael asked me while passing by my desk.

Maybe he'd noticed the same shirt that I'd been wearing since three days, or maybe my ruffled hair and thick stubble was becoming noticeable now.

I said yes and passed him the reports I'd prepared.

"You finished them all? All of them?" he asked looking at them in surprise.

"Let me get them validated. You can leave for the day, see you tomorrow." He continued.

"I'll do it. It's just eight. I'll leave after sometime" I said and took the reports from him without waiting for his reply.

"Are you sure you're alright?" he asked again, this time sounding more concerned.

"Yes. I'll do it Michael. I'll do it all. Just leave me alone."

3

I'LL HIT YOU SO HARD, ALL YOUR PLANS WILL FAIL

My usual routine included working till midnight and then smoking marijuana at home.

I used to find the cab driver in deep sleep and asked him to stay at office and used to bring back his car in the morning.

At work, I smoked several packs of cigarettes and rarely talked to anyone.

I'd slowly found a way out in marijuana and by keeping myself busy in work. I don't know what a junkie is, but I used to smoke up no less than ten joints a day, on weekends, I smoked hash, with Raja and Balu, my cab driver, staying over at my place.

I used to get up coughing hard in the middle of the night, and spat black and thick phlegm repeatedly everyday.

People at office said I looked thin and gauntly, but then they always had something more important to talk in form of work, and so I never let myself think in that direction.

Sometimes, I opened that picture and just looked at it, she and the white guy, both of them smiling at me, I deliberately didn't take my eyes off it and used to feel the horror slowly creeping over my body. After a few minutes, I used to smoke up and pass out.

Days went by and I started accepting things by almost never being sober.

I learned to work, make reports, talk to clients, even when I was stoned.

It made my mind function in just one direction and not wander into random thoughts.

I barely looked into the mirror but I knew I was a mess, my collar bones were starkly visible, and my eyes were almost always bloodshot.

One day, I was smoking a joint standing in the open area of office with Raja when someone patted on my shoulder from behind, I turned around to see. It was Michael.

He came forward and smelled the joint in my hand, "Alley, I want to see you in my office, now", he said and left.

There was silence, Raja looked at me jaw dropped. After a zoned out minute it struck me that I was about to be fired. I was too stoned to understand the situation completely. I finished the remaining joint and went to meet Michael.

"Can I enter?" I said opening the door of his cabin.

"Hey Alley, come sit." he said signalling at a chair.

"See Michael, I know what I was doing there is wrong, moreover illegal, I apologize for that. Please don't book a case, let me resign myself" I said trying hard to speak clearly but failing at it.

"What makes you think I would agree to that?" he said looking straight at me.

"You go out and do your work for now. I'll talk to you later" he continued and went back to his monitor.

Getting booked under possession of marijuana was a punishable offense.

I'd have easily paid a few thousand rupees and escaped, but a case filed from your employer assures your way to prison, atleast for a month.

Thinking of all this, suddenly a moment of realisation struck me, I was sitting in front of EnY India head, messed up and only half sober, caught smoking marijuana with the office peon, and now pleading him to save me from police.

I decided that my fate was sealed now, Michael isn't gonna let me go easily.

I got up and came to my desk.

I tried to finish all my work that day, with joblessness, handcuffs and a dark Indian prison cell in my mind.

Michael kept hovering around my desk, probably to make sure I won't leave and abscond.

I began to think about my rented apartment that I'd have to lose and my side of the story that I'll have to tell the law officials, I wouldn't have a lawyer, I'd rot in jail and last I read there are rampant killings and sodomy in Bangalore central prison.

There would be some prisoners who'd have hashish, will they give a little to me? What will they ask in return? And will the police give me a chance to inform at home that I'm going on a vacation in jail, and if they do give me the phone in police station, who'd be the first person I'd want to call? Will they let me make a call to the US, so that I can inform someone how I ended up, and how unpredictably funny life can be.

"Alley, come in!" suddenly Michael's voice broke my train of thoughts. I saw him going into his cabin.

It was 8.30, I'd a lot of work to be done and had already left footnotes under each of my reports to enable the new guy understand them easily.

I understood that Michael would be leaving now and this might be the last time I'd see him, and would get to see my desk.

Will they take me in handcuffs? Will Michael really call the cops here in office, or he might just tell me to sign on my resignation.

I opened the door and asked him permission to come in.

"Come sit, and just listen to me" he said signalling towards the chair while going through my reports.

"Your reports, your work, I've no complaints from that. Infact it's fabulous, you stay in office till midnight and do the validator's work too, which again is great. Why should I fire you then? Shouldn't I fire that validator guy for not doing anything?"

"Shut up," he said before I could answer, "there is a difference tough, he doesn't smoke marijuana in office, you do. Now tell me why shouldn't I fire you?"

I didn't speak a word and just dropped my head in shame.

"Tell me one thing, what is it?" he said after a pause.

"What is what?" I asked in reflex, suddenly realising I was an estranged employee on the verge of being fired by his boss, and probably booked, I lowered my voice and said sorry.

"Till a month back, you headed out of office sharp at five. I barely saw you smoking in that area. Now, all you do is smoke and dig your head in these goddamn reports. Look at you man, you used to be neat, today your clothes aren't even ironed, your eyes are bloodshot most of the times. See, that ink blot on your shirt pocket, it's getting bigger everyday. You do hell lotta more work than you should do, so I have no reason to be fire you or even to care about your well being, but you're young and smart, what is so wrong and terrible about your life that you're treating yourself like this? Don't answer if it's personal, but let me tell you something, you need to get yourself together. Not your work, but yourself."

That evening, instead of ending up in prison, I ended up telling Michael everything about Divya.

That was the first time I disclosed my agony to anyone.

I told him how I perfectly fit in the image of a dumped lover and how I still was getting to terms with losing her like this.

He suddenly cut me midway and said, "Your story is funny, forget all this crap"

"What?" I asked in shock.

He didn't answer me and said, "You need to party. You need to meet new people and have fun. You know, meet girls and all." he said winking at me.

"It's not like that Michael"

"It is. Today's Friday, go catch a nice party in Bangalore." He said standing up and getting ready to leave.

"No it's okay. Anyways, thanks for not firing me" I said looking at him and smiled.

"Get over it man, you were dumped, that's about it. Look at me, I too was dumped, and not just by my wife but by my kids too." He said and left, shutting the door of his cabin behind him.

Sitting there, I let out a sigh of relief for still having my job. I went out and found Raja standing near my desk.

"What did he say? Everything okay?" he came rushing towards me.

"You were right, he is actually the Mai-ka-lal here." I said and put my arm around his shoulders. He laughed and what followed was a mind-boggling series of Hindi expletives.

✿✿

My doorbell rings repeatedly and I wake up from a deep sleep.

I look around, I'm in my room. I look at the clock, it's seven in the evening. I slowly recollect that it's Saturday and I'd a heavy dope of hashish in the morning with Raja and Balu.

The doorbell again pierces through my head. I struggled to get up and notice another drone of music, Jimi Hendrix's "Castles Made of Sand" has been playing in loop since morning.

I force myself to rise from the bed, my body is lost somewhere and my head feels like floating midair.

I try to walk upright through the hall and open the main door.

"Ali bhai!" somebody pushed me and barged into the house. I know the voice, it's Balu.

"Ali bhai. Are you still high? I've to take you somewhere" he said helping me get back to my room.

"Where?" I said and veiled my eyes as he switched on the lights.

"Mai-ka-lal called me. Here. On my cellphone." He said flashing his mobile phone towards me.

"So?"

"He called me on my cellphone Ali bhai! Mai-ka-lal called on my personal cellphone!" He exclaimed almost shouting and again flashed his phone towards me.

"Keep that in your pocket and tell me what he said" I asked signalling him to sit.

"He knows a lot about you Ali bhai. He knows that you smoke *ganja* in office" He continued shouting without caring to sit.

"I know that. What else did he say?"

"He blackmailed me with that and I'd to tell him everything" he said suddenly lowering his voice.

"What?" I sprang up from my bed.

"I'd to tell him that we smoke hashish here in your room"

"WHAT?!"

"But I told him we never smoked it in office, except just once, and that too we went to the terrace for that, not in the balcony."

"What are you saying Balu? What the fuck!" I said and clenched my head, trying to get sober.

"What did he say?" I asked him after a minute of silence.

"He said I've to take you out"

"What?"

"I mean he told me I've to drive you to a party, otherwise he'll fire me"

"Party?"

"Yes, he's given me address of some party happening in a farmhouse in outskirts. I've to take you there"

"Listen, tell him we went to the party, let's go and get some stuff" I told and collapsed on my bed again.

"No, he said you've to go, even he's coming there"

"What? Michael's also going?"

"Yes, and he said I've to make you wear good clothes, make you shave and even make you take a shower. I relented but Ali bhai, please do all this on your own, I really can't do this kind of work"

"Shut up" I said and went to the restroom.

Balu drove for almost an hour to the address Michael had given him.

Shaving seemed too much of work to me especially with the hash still having its effect, but I did take a hot shower and wore black shirt and black tie, the dress code that Michael had texted me.

We reached the farmhouse after much effort from nearby vendors and highway teashops, Michael never answered my call due to the loud music.

"You go Ali bhai, I'll wait here" Balu said as we reached the porch of the grand bungalow where the party was going on.

"What will you do here? It'll take very long." I asked getting down from the car.

"I'll sleep in the car, or if you can send something from inside, I'll party here with other drivers" he said with a wide grin.

"Why can't you just come inside? Park the car somewhere and come"

"No Ali bhai, these parties are not for us, I'm okay outside, and more over they'll never let me go inside"

"Sneaking you inside would be much easier than sneaking stuff outside, now go and park the car, I'm waiting here" I said and got out of the car.

Balu returned after parking the car, reluctant about heading towards the entrance to the party. I pushed him towards the entrance and turned away. Two thugs dressed in black blocked the door. They held a paper which was probably the guest list.

After a plan and much persuasion, I told Balu to call himself Ali, cos I knew my name was there in the list. It worked, they checked my name and instantly allowed him inside, he went in looking at me with a wide grin 'cause it was probably the first time he was not waiting outside a party but was actually getting inside it.

I went in next, "Sir, your name please?" one of the bouncers asked me with a hoarse voice.

"I don't think it'll be there on the guest list, I got an invite for this party pretty late" I said trying to sound smooth.

"Sir then I don't think we can allow you inside" He'd have probably lifted me three feet up in the air the moment I said my name wasn't in the list, but with my black shirt and tie and elite demeanour that I was faking, I didn't look like a wannabe party hopper at first glance and he was still talking to me.

"I've got friends inside buddy, you want me to call the organiser here?" I said passing a thousand rupee note into his hand.

With a slight smile on his face, he cleared my way.

The door opened and the slow drone of music suddenly became full blasted.

I moved in and suddenly someone came forward and hugged me tightly, I tried to see the face in the dark, it was Balu.

He was saying something but 'Ali bhai' was all I could hear. I signalled him towards the bar and asked him not to pass out and not worry about driving.

I suddenly realised there was no dress code, I was probably the only person dressed in shirt and tie.

I looked around and found Michael near the bar, the India head of EnY was wearing a flimsy t-shirt bearing the text 'Get out my way, bitch!', over shorts and flipflops, with his big round tummy accentuating out of the shirt.

"My man!" he shouted on seeing me with his beer mug raised up in the air.

Even considering the music around, he was loud and growly, and attracted a few glances towards me.

He stood up and walked towards me, his steps were bigger and there was no corporate élan, he looked like a rough beer gutted bald man walking down the road.

"Alley my man!" he patted hard on my shoulder and looked at a girl standing next to me.

Before I could say anything, he moved forward towards his friends pushing me aside.

I went towards the bar, picked up a drink and sought a corner to park myself for the rest of the party.

"Hey" I heard a female voice whispering into my ear from behind.

I turned around to find a girl with an anorexic body, probably a fake bosom and a skimpy, shining black dress covering it.

"What's up?" she shouted towards me slowly shaking her body with the music.

She was tipsy and probably wanted someone to buy her drinks. I smiled at her and turned back.

"Hey" she shouted again and I again turned at her and smiled.

"You want blotters?" she asked just as I was about to turn back.

I'd a long look at her and asked, "What's that?"

"LSD blotters kid. Acid. Try it. They're awesome." she said fishing out a strip of small colourful square patterns from her pocket.

I had heard about LSD before, and that it alters the thinking processes, I looked around to catch a glimpse of Balu. He was still at the same spot, with a drink in his hand and chatting away with the bartender.

"Just place it on your tongue and think nothing of it. Like this." she said suddenly coming towards me and placed a small patch out of the strip on her tongue.

I looked at the patch suddenly discolouring on the surface of her tongue. She suddenly tripped towards me making me step forward to give her support. I tried to sit her down on the couch nearby.

On the risk of altering my already altered thinking process, I relented to trying a LSD blotter as she thrust the strip in my hand. I carefully detached one small piece of paper from the strip and placed it on my tongue. In a few seconds the party seemed like a fusion of colours and music to me.

I tried to stretch my eyes and gain consciousness but in vain. I deciphered from my badly disfigured vision that she was smiling at me and lighting something in a glass pipe that she constantly kept trying to pass on to me.

Next thing I knew, I was smoking a meth crystal through a glass-pipe, mistaking it for regular hash.

The shots of dense smoke from the pipe concocted with the LSD gave me a mind numbing impact, there were bouts of absolute darkness followed by sudden visuals of the party which now looked like a confusing mixture of colours and music.

I started forgetting things, where I was and what had brought me here on this couch, I'd to convince my mind into thinking that I was alive and my head was still affixed to my body.

All I could understand was that there was some weight thrown all over my body and a sharp fragrance was entering my nose.

I suddenly felt my hands groping and fumbling the weight vigorously and realised it was this girl.

I try to balk and shake her off but at the same time I had my hands going into her dress.

She repeatedly kissed me to an extent of almost biting my lips, every time passing some strong alcoholic drink from her mouth into mine.

I could understand that it was some strong spirit making me go haywire, and it sure was making my testosterone shoot up every time I swigged it.

I suddenly gained some perception when her hand crept through my trousers and caught hold of my crotch.

"Lady what are you doing!" I tried to shout but all I could hear was some wobbly mixture of words.

Probably seeing me getting worked up and panicked, she came down to my ear and whispered, "Your place or mine?" that was the first thing I heard clearly after a long time.

"Leave me alone!" I tried to shout back.

"Don't worry, I'll take you to my place" she whispered in my ear and again passed a heavy swig of the liquid into my mouth.

Either the liquid got stuck in my throat making me lose my breath, or it went up my nostrils, but that very moment I got a jolt of consciousness.

I pushed her away trying to shout towards her but she resisted hard.

"Bitch, get off me! I don't wanna make out!" I shouted in her ear as loud as I could and pushed her so hard that she toppled from the couch.

Regaining whatever energy I had in my body, I got up and fastened my zipper.

My shirt was untucked and wet with spit and alcohol.

I recollected myself and tried to look out for the exit when suddenly a piercing shriek cut through my ears.

"You bastard! Sonofabitch! What is wrong with you? Get the fuck out of here!" I turned around to find her shouting at me with her eyes wide open. The glass in her hand came flying at me and I ducked at just the right moment with more alcohol spilling on my shirt.

The bouncer came and stood next to me and the music suddenly stopped with the sharp sound of glass shattering on the floor.

"Sir, you better leave right away or we'll have to escort you out," he whispered into my ear.

"Alright, I'm outta here" I announced with my hands raised and smiled at all the faces staring at me. I was still high.

With a throbbing head, I tried to control my walk towards the doorway.

At a corner, I could see Michael looking at me in disgust just when I had reached the door.

The music resumed as the door behind me closed leaving me out in the cold breeze.

I walked to the parking and sat in Balu's car waiting for some sobriety.

My breath and clothes reeked of the spirit I had swigged and spilled all over me.

There were no cops on the long highway connecting to the city, I lit a cigarette, started the car and sped away with a screech.

After reaching the city I diverted the car and took the usual turn towards the long elevated highway, to burn rubber and probably looking for a vent to burn away the bitterness of the night.

Though I had lost count of how many times I sped hard on this straight stretch of asphalt with the darkness of the night and thick Marlboro smoke surrounding me, the moment never failed to pull me in the introspection mode that I always come here looking for. And this night, like so many others, deserved one.

I pulled the car to the side of the road and lit a marijuana joint I'd found in the dashboard.

I noticed my shirt slowly drying up by the wind and decided to stand there for a while.

Though the smoke going in killed the taste of the foul liquid, the shouting face of the fake bosom girl was still clear in my mind, and so was Michael's repulsive expression when I was leaving.

Under me was the long road that led to Bangalore College of Engineering, I thought of the times me and Sandy used to speed our bike on this road, high on a concoction of weed and life.

Loosening the knot of my tie and dragging more smoke in, I could see myself riding my long abandoned rusty RX 100 on the other end of the road.

Like always, there's Sandy on the pillion seat, and though the bike's drone is deafening both of us out, we both are shouting at each other knowing none of us is audible.

I noticed tears in my eyes, and suddenly, beyond my control, my mind freshened up all the thoughts of Divya, Sandy, and the life I'd left behind on this highway.

The Ali on the bike suddenly looked at me, his gaze sharp and mocking. He shakes his head and smiles at my helplessness.

I get a saddening realisation that I'm no more him, I'm someone else now, far away from that life and I could do nothing to get it back.

I wonder what had got me here, leaning on the parapet of a flyover at three o clock in the night and hallucinating the life I'd left behind.

I'd nothing left in life other than desperation and helplessness, I just wanted more weed and more hash, and even more reports and more work. I questioned myself where was I heading this way. No one responded.

I called up Balu.

I woke up late in the afternoon the next day.

Balu was sleeping in the hall, and I still had my smelling shirt and tie on.

I gulped down a water of bottle to relieve my throat which was parched from long drags of meth smoke the night before.

After a warm shower and shaving off my thick stubble, I showed up in office. Michael called me to his cabin.

"You created a ruckus yesterday you idiot!" he said just as I entered.

"I'm sorry. I didn't mean to create any scene"

"You pushed that girl to the floor! Were you out of your mind?" he said raising his tone.

"Yes, that's kind of true actually. And you don't know anything that happened there Mike. So it'd be better if we drop this here and start some work."

"I know everything! Who do you think sent her behind you? I paid her man." He said and suddenly paused.

"What? You what?" I asked him exclaimed.

He walked up to me and asked me to sit down, "See Alley, I'm sorry about that but..."

"But what? Was she a hooker? Christ's sake! You think I'm looking for paid sex? What is wrong with you Michael? You could have atleast asked me once!" I said and without waiting for him to answer, exited his cabin saying, "Listen Michael, let's not talk about this again"

Sitting on my desk, I looked at my reflection in the dead monitor, and wondered had I started to come across as a sex starved man.

I sure did look like a junkie, though in little neater clothes. When I looked at myself after shaving off my stubble, like right now, I was reluctant to accept that I'd lost weight from my face too, my eyes looked poppy, and my spectacles had started to look over sized.

I thought to myself that I'll stop smoking up, and suddenly very next moment something trebled inside me telling me that it was impossible.

Then I thought I will cut down, then the same trebling told me how will the evening pass otherwise, and that the option again was impossible.

Once I told myself that there's more hashish and more weed joints waiting for me at home, I was at peace.

I realised maybe this is what people called dependency, the next stage of addiction, and that shook me up.

I was not able to tell myself that I'd grown dependent on the substances, and couldn't either tell myself that I will never do it again from this moment on.

There were no people left in my life, except two middle aged office clerks whom I bribed with free hash into hanging out with me.

I open my facebook page everyday, and see hundreds of people online, they all have so much to say and so much to talk about.

I always tried to find one topic of interest which I could delve into, but there was nothing.

My mind did a lot of work, reports and validations all day long, but at end of the day, there was nothing, nothing I could figure out, I was coming to a realisation that I was just alive, hollowing myself from the core, by marijuana and memories, both of which had run out my control now.

I also realised, still staring blankly into my dead monitor, that I'd also become wildly restless, I always wanted to lay down on my bed, but whenever I did so, I felt an urge to sit up straight. I wanted to cry, but whenever I locked myself up and cried, I wanted to stop and do something else.

I thought of leaving office early and got up, but just as I walked away, I realised I'd nothing else to do, at home or otherwise, I sat back again.

I was a fuck up, a recluse with whom people wouldn't want to talk to, my boss looked down upon me as a sex starved, messed up employee, and others sitting around me just knew my name, and that I finished work in time, they also knew I was someone who was either at his desk or smoking at the terrace, who wore crumbled shirts and always had drowsy eyes, they could use me well in their luncheon gossips, beyond that I didn't matter to anyone around.

I thought about death, and it terrified me again, I wanted to live, and doubted if I could get back to living anytime soon. I called up Sandy.

4

LIFE STRIKES YOU. IT DOES

"What the fuck!" this is what the person standing in front of me shouted when I answered the door bell one early morning.

He was Sandy.

"Oh God! Sandy, is that you?" I asked rubbing my eyes.

"Get aside sucker! Look at you! What the fuck have you been doing?" he said pushing me aside and entered in.

I was confused, I'd called Sandy three days ago and had abruptly disconnected the call just before I broke down. I waited for him to call back, and like always, he didn't. But I think he heard me weeping when I disconnected, and here he was.

Amid all the confusion, I also noticed something else, all the weight I'd lost had probably transferred to him, in form of muscles.

His biceps bulged out of his tshirt sleeves, and right now in front of him, I felt a sudden shame and disgust upon myself.

We both had the same eight months to ourselves after college, while he was in Goa and I here. And here we were meeting again, looking at him, I felt I'd lost something I'll never get back, and before I could say anything, he came forward and hugged me tight.

"What have you done to yourself bitch!" he said while I felt almost crushed in his arms.

It was a shocker for me, there were times when I used to be so high that I hallucinated things. I thought hard to myself, this all was indeed happening. I hugged him back and smiled, it was after months that I'd hugged anyone, if the fake bosom girl in the party wasn't counted.

"Now get off me, and carry in my luggage" he said and picked up his huge backpack.

"Why didn't you tell me?" I asked picking up his other bag.

"Tell you what?" he asked.

"That you'd come, this is such a shocker"

"There's a lot to tell, wait here, I'll just come" he said and went out of the house.

I settled his luggage in the other room and took a sigh of relief, seeing Sandy was shocking and exhilarating at the same time.

I didn't know whether he had come here for a few days or for long. The past few minutes were probably the best I'd felt since months.

"What are you doing? Come out you ass" he said suddenly entering the room where I was settling his luggage.

"What happened?" I asked coming out.

"Meet her" he said signalling towards a girl.

It was again a shocker. A tall, golden haired blonde, probably American, stood in front of me.

A close look at her told me that she was a hippie, her smile showed her tobacco stained teeth, and her attire was a khadi shirt and wrap around, with wood beaded necklaces around her neck and her rough hair tied in a big bun.

"Well, uh, hello there" I said recovering from the initial shock.

"Hi. You must be, uh, Ali" she said dropping down her big backpack.

"Yes, and you are?"

"I'm Holika" she said shaking my hand and lit a cigarette, I noticed they were hand made ones, raw tobacco rolled into rolling paper at home, which well explained her stained teeth.

"Holika? Nice name. But doesn't that sound a little Indian" I said as she offered me a cigarette from the metal case in which they were kept.

"Little Indian? Dude! Holika is Sanskrit. She was a demoness who was burnt to death on the day of Holi. Her death signifies victory of good over evil. Too bad they don't know she still exists", she said puffing smoke from her mouth.

"Wow! Alright Holika, nice to meet you" I said blown away by the sudden gust of knowledge, and didn't care to ask her real name, which I'm sure she'd have abandoned long back.

"And Holika, find a place to stay in this huge house. It is all ours, and best thing, it's free!" Sandy said announcing it towards me and her.

"Wow! Thanks Ali" she said and sat down on the floor to unpack her backpack, seemingly unaffected by my shocked face.

I pulled Sandy in the other room and asked, "What's going on? Who's she? And why would she stay here?"

"Let's put her in this room, you and me can stay in your room" he said completely ignoring all my questions, "Holy cow! Look at this mess" he said entering my room.

"Sandy, who's she?" I asked him again following him to my room.

"She's Holika, and there's a lot to tell" he said and smiled.

✿✿

After that phonecall from me, Sandy instantnly decided to leave behind Goa, his dad's steel plant, his villa, his six dogs, but not Holika, whom he'd met at a beach shack one day. I later got to know they liked to call themselves just friends, a 'friendship' that had started with 'your place or mine?' and was now at my place.

Holika was 'a chick full of philosophical crap', this is how Sandy had first described her.

The tattoos on her arm ranged from the American eagle to an Om and a Swastika, which well defined her journey to India, which she now called home.

She and Sandy had been staying together for six months now. I knew they shared a deep bond, which went beyond casual sex, it reflected in their eyes, but it always got lost in our loud laughter and crazy times together.

When I told Sandy about Divya, he'd nothing to say, he smiled and told me he knew it had happened, it reflected in my voice over the phone, but that day when I cried before disconnecting the call, he packed his bags and set out to Bangalore.

He played the same Eminem song on blasting volume that

we used to play in our hostel room, and again did his random moves that he used to call dance.

'But I guess that's just what sluts do,
How could it ever be just us two?
I never loved you enough to trust you,
We just met and I just fucked you.

He called this his break up therapy, I didn't know if it worked, but seeing Sandy dance bought back all the college memories.

We shared the room same way like in college, and Holika stayed in the other room.

Sandy used to show around the city to Holika while I went to office, and I started spending limited hours in office, giving validator some of my work to make up for the months of work I did for him.

I now had people to talk to, I even used to cook for the three of us, me, Sandy and Holika. And now, I didn't cry in the bathroom or thought about death, I just laughed and worked out in the evenings with Sandy.

He made me run on the treadmill till I almost lost breath, and forced raw eggs with milk down my throat.

Holika used to smoke up hash sometimes in the house, but Sandy never let me touch it. I sometimes even tried to shout at him, but he never relented into letting me even inhale the smoke, so that I don't get the urge.

"Weed is a bitch, and a deadly one at that, and bitches should better be kept leashed or they leash you soon", he once said when I'd asked him the reason for stopping me from smoking up.

I knew I had overdone it, but he hadn't, and so it was normal that he always wanted to smoke up with Holika, but months went by and he too never touched it, so that I don't feel left out and pathetic.

I later figured out I could have gone to the point of no return if he hadn't showed up on my door that day.

Sandy had again left a void my making 'thank you' seem too trivial and small for what he had done for me. And though I tried thanking him many times, he never let me do it, and always had something petty to laugh about or if nothing would figure up, he'd swear at Holika in rash Hindi slang and we both would burst out laughing, while she just stared.

It had been three months since Sandy and Holika had come to stay with me, and today was Holika's birthday, or more precisely, the day she had come to India, which she later started celebrating as her birthday and chose to forget the real date of her birth.

'Hippies don't just smoke up and wander the streets in flipflops, they've a long story behind them, all of it abandoned in search of a moment of freedom. And from what I've heard, they never get it, though I'm staying positive on this' Holika had once told me, winking on the last line.

Most of her philosophy on life and existence went beyond my intellect, she'd grave, serious thoughts about the things of the universe and the purpose of life.

Sometimes she'd just sit in the balcony for hours and scribble something in her diary. But beyond all of it, I could see the persona of a naughty playful girl whose life had turned around in the moment of someone else's actions.

I'd a lot of questions to ask her, but I never asked anything, because I knew she'd never tell me anything. I wasn't even a small part of her life, to her, I was the guy who stayed in the room across hers and who made nice coffee and omelette when there was no maid in the house.

I left office early that evening, and bought a backpack for Holika as her gift, I put a few philosophical novels in it, ones which I knew she hadn't read yet.

I wondered how she'll find it, Holika was the kind of girl who can make you look like a dumbass or a superman in a single moment.

It was hard for me to decipher whether she'd like something which she could utilise as a gift, or something that she could just keep with her.

Sandy had kept it simple, he hadn't bought anything, wish I could do that too.

I entered the house to find only Sandy, he told me Holika had gone out somewhere, and would be returning with her friends later in the night.

I quietly kept the bag in her room and went to work out with Sandy. Holika came home late in the night, with around dozen people, most of them non-Indians.

They were a boisterous group, talking amongst themselves in mix of English and Italian and some language which I couldn't understand.

Nobody particularly cared about meeting me, but most of them went and talked to Sandy, some couldn't even speak fluent English, but they still went and met him, and Holika smiled all through as they did so, translating in English what they had to say to Sandy.

They'd got a huge chocolate cake which everyone binged on, and lot of booze and hash with them.

Eventually they all started speaking in Italian, and me and Sandy got cornered out.

Some of them weren't drinking, but each one of them smoked hash in turns, and Sandy let me join them. I got a chance to smoke up after more than three months, with Sandy sitting right next to me so that I don't overdo it.

I smoked up many joints that night, all in turns, taking few puffs and passing it over to Sandy.

The room was going loud with shouts and laughter of the group, and just when my vision had started getting blurred and I thought the night was over, the girl sitting next to me, who was passing me the joint and spoke only occasionally, turned towards me for the first time and asked me in broken English, "So what's your name?".

I tried to squint my eyes and take a clear look of her face. They say life strikes you at most unexpected of times, and they say right. Because just like that, sitting in that overcrowded room, almost passing out on hash, and trying to find words for an answer to that Italian woman, life struck me.

"A, uh, a, Ali... My name's Ali." I said in an English far more broken than hers.

"I'm Christa." she said and smiled.

5

CHRISTA SPEAKS

When you come out of the New Delhi Airport in white skin, people hound you. That was my first sight of India.

I had never imagined that the small green colour shape labelled 'India' on the world-map could pack in so many people. All moving. All shouting. All at once.

The sun in New Delhi comes down and sits over your head in the month of May, and amid that when you walk out with your eyes wandering and a Delhi map in your hand, tens of hairy men run at you like they'll eat you up in one gobble.

"Madam! Me full English, giving full good service, giving good hotel giving good taxi giving good food. Giving full enjoy in India. Come madam," a man with a strange turban and dense beard shouted towards me pushing a crowd of others aside.

I knew he was trying hard at the English language, but I had to try harder to respond.

"I no good money. I needing cheap hotel, clean hotel," I called out to the whole mob.

Most of them argued with each other, remaining few fought it out to grab hold of my luggage trolley, and others were just expressionless onlookers, amid all the chaos, they managed to continuously look at my breasts.

Suddenly a police officer emerged out of nowhere, having a force in his voice that brushed the mob aside instantly.

"Madam, where you going?" he asked me with a sudden but forced politeness in his voice.

"I tourist. I needing cheap and clean hotel" I told him.

"No problem madam. I giving you hotel where you finding many Amreekans, all like you, having enjoy in India. India welcome all Amreekans" he said and shook my hands.

He signalled something to the turban man and got me a prepaid taxi slip. It had a destination address named 'Paharganj'. Back then, I knew nothing about the place, today, I can guide the taxi driver into alleys of Paharganj that he never knew existed.

I figured out that the taxi driver had an innate ability of talking to people without getting any reply, and the rear view mirror of his car served another purposes than the one I knew it does.

I learned one thing from him, to speak English confidently, by using just a few words from the language in all possible combinations.

"This India gate, all people dying in wars writing names on this. My relative name also Madam"

"This Red Fort, prime minister come and doing talking

on fifteen august. Full good talking under the big India flag Madam. You see must. Call me I take you"

"This Taj Hotel, you doing drinking and dancing? Come to here, it having all Amreekan people doing dances and drinking and laughing full night."

"This your place Paharganj" he said finally as the destination printed on the prepaid ticket arrived.

It was a lane full of roadside motels, with narrow illuminated display boards scaled aside each one of them. I could see non Indians roaming aimlessly and chatting at eateries. That gave me a little relief.

The driver drove by a motel named 'Hotel Yes Please', I smiled looking at the name, which was probably the first time I smiled in India, "Stop there please" I asked him pointing at the hotel.

"Oh that very good hotels, giving good food and good rooms" he said before I stepped out of the car.

A guy from hotel came running down the stairs and grabbed my luggage to carry it in. The driver asked hundred rupees extra over the prepaid bill I'd already paid, the guy from the hotel shouted some tongue twisting words towards him, which I now know as Hindi curse words, and he was gone.

The man at the reception asked me my nationality, and gave me a room on the floor which had more people from my country.

The room was small, but had everything, a bed, television, AC and a small bathroom that just served the purpose.

I threw myself on the bed and let out a big sigh.

It was a moment of relief, and with that, starts my story.

I must introduce myself now, I'm Christa, and when twelve Italians arrived in India looking for a cheap party spot, I don't know why they were stupid enough to carry cocaine in their hand bags at the airport.

I also don't know why my country, Italy, sent me as the official diplomat to get them extradited. Now let me make one thing clear, when twelve hippies get stuck in a third world country, a country such as mine treats them dead.

When their relatives come knocking on the government's door too very often, they pick up a young, low earning intern like me and throw them on a plane to the country.

A huge pile of case files and the address of the Italian embassy is all that they give you, and last I heard, they treat you dead too.

I looked at the slowly rotating ceiling fan, hearing its strange creaking sound in monotony with its every rotation.

Today when I think of it, it gives me a perfect memory of India, flashbacking each event with its each creaking rotation.

Now when you're a new-on-the-job intern and when your boss comes and asks you, "Do you have your passport ready?". You'd exhilarate, thinking you're getting a chance to go and work abroad, which would mean exploring a new country.

I was no different, when my department head asked me for my passport status, I instantly replied with a positive.

"Well Christa, its India for you. Airport arrest, twelve nationals, same old drugs' hassle" he said fishing out an old stack of files which had a band over them that said 'Priority: Low'. If they'd their way, they'd have put that band over me too.

Just before I left the cabin, he said getting up from his chair, "As you're still not on payroll, all your reimbursements shall be processed after an year, so for now manage your money well"

Before I could react, that is come up with a shocked face, he had left.

Soon after, I found myself in India, and now under this creaking ceiling fan.

Now let me make one more thing clear, when Indians see a fair skinned young girl walking down the streets, they need to let go four misconceptions about her. One, they all have money in sacks. Two, they all know good English. Three, they all are *amreekans.* And four, all they do is have sex and smoke hash all day long.

When I came to India, my money was running out every hour, I was an Italian with my English in scraps, and was practicing celibacy. Hash was a distant dream, but then little I knew about Paharganj.

First thing the service boy knocking at my hotel room asked me was that whether I wanted stuff, any stuff, he said, weed, hash, ecstacy, shrooms, crack or acid.

He was a teenaged boy with fluent English, and a well rehearsed menu of the 'stuff' he sold.

He left me jaw dropped that day, but today, I can leave him jaw dropped, with my English and a bigger list of stuff that I can get him.

Paharganj was a hippie haven, in the scorching summer sun, when I walked out of my hotel for lunch, there were German Bakeries lining the network of streets, most of them having hippies dressed in scrap clothing and smoking joints.

I ate pasta, which tasted strange, I later got to know as that strange taste as the taste of a typical Indian curry.

Walking back to my room, willing to open up some case documents and start reading them, same errand boy met me again at the hotel staircase. He looked at me for a moment and slipped his hands down the pockets of his rugged knickers, as if searching for something, "here's some hash for you, roll up and enjoy madam" he said and passed me a small hash ball as if it were a candy.

I smelled it suspecting it to be some tourist looting dope, but I don't know what triggered me from within, I rolled up the stuff with tobacco in a Gold flake cigarette and smoked it up.

Again staring at the creaking fan, stomach full and high this time, here I was, I thought to myself, a foreign diplomat, high on free hash and lying in a cheap hotel four thousand miles away from my country, to rescue a set of people who were caught carrying illegal narco. I laughed.

"Anywhere you get stuck in India, all you've to do is flash this" the official in the Italian embassy gave me a diplomatic pass, which would be my entry ticket to any Indian government office, my driving licence, and my only identity that worked in in India.

I had to go to Delhi Airport police and track down the victims myself, until I didn't do that, he told me I don't need to show up in the embassy again.

It was my second day at Delhi, and I woke up late in my Paharganj hotel, my itinerary said that I've to go to Delhi Airport Police station today, but I'd all the time in the world.

I walked to the narrow, sunlight deprived gallery of my hotel which had many rooms aligning it.

On the small window at the far end, there was a girl smoking cigarette and looking out.

She'd ruffled, brown hair, and shabby clothing, she looked uninviting but I needed company, so I went and talked to her.

"Hi" I said finding a place to stand next to her.

"Hi" she said glancing at me for a moment.

"What are you doing in India?" I asked as she went back to looking out of the window.

"Nothing. You?" she said blowing smoke.

I thought for a moment, and realised my story was a long and boring one to be told to her, "Nothing" I replied and she smiled at me.

"Ann" she said and shook hands with me.

Ann stayed in the room next to me, and gradually I realised everybody had their particular 'nothing' to do in Paharganj. They roamed the streets to Delhi all day, did strange jobs, and mostly did nothing, their *nothing.*

My nothing was playing a police-station-hopping-clueless-diplomat, and soon it became Ann's nothing too.

"Your dressing makes you look rich. And that's a big mistake to do in India" Ann once told me.

She gave me a fat novel about an Australian convict's runaway life in India, 'Shantaram', it was a bulky book and it taught me mainly two things, English and surviving in India.

My quest for chasing my case was haywire and random.

Policemen usually had no clue about what I was talking about when I showed them photographs of twelve foreigners and reference numbers of old case files.

"Come tomorrow, to talk to the *saab*" was the usual reply I got.

Newspapers told me that there were nearly thirty million cases pending in Indian courts, and I wondered will I ever be able to track my case out of that number.

I was liking India, but not to the extent of staying here forever.

"Hey my ladies" Fred called out towards me and Ann entering the eatery where we sat.

Fred was an American by skin and Indian by flesh guy.

He came to India a decade ago, for a vacation in Goa, and never returned. With an expired Visa and expired sense of belonging to America, Fred was a Paharganj peddler now.

He did everything for money, or let me put it this way, everything he did was for money.

He peddled drugs, bandaged infected injection wounds when addicts couldn't afford a doctor and wanted to stay out of drugs' trouble, supplied girls, and even had sex, with men and women, all for money.

He came and sat on the chair opposite to ours, and started narrating a story, "Whoa man, today crazy scene at the airport. Wild turtles caught at the terminal, my guy had to pay fuckin three hundred grands to get them out"

"Airport? Like Delhi airport?" I asked him.

"Yeah, that's the only one around I guess" he said pulling my pasta towards him.

"Oh my Freddy boy, you gotta help me out"

I struck me that having a hinglish speaking fellow expat knowing his way around in a new country would help me immensely, and thus I told Fred about the case and how I was low on money as well as devoid of any contacts in this country. He clearly stated that he would need certain amount for each piece of information he might get to me related to the case. I found it kind of shocking back then, but today, I feel it was just astute business, and it's very important not to mix business with anything else in India.

After a few days, Fred started getting me details of the case. Whenever he went to the airport, he got me a new detail.

"They say they were first jailed in Delhi but now are transferred to Bangalore" he said one day.

"What? Bangalore? What's that?" I asked him.

"It's a city. Far from here. Very far. In southern part of India. You've a map?"

That put me on a plane to Bangalore, and funny that life is, in a new city, and I'd a new nothing to do.

A nothing that led me to prisons and parties.

My first party at Bangalore, where I was invited by an Italian friend, was at a farmhouse far off from the city.

It was a loud and dark party, with many non Indians around. I was sitting on a couch at a corner of a room when a girl and a young Indian guy took the rest of the couch.

The girl looked nasty and caked up with makeup.

She was a hooker, by now I could recognize them in a moment.

She lit some meth crystals through a glass pipe and offered the guy, trying to lean over him. He looked dazed and restless and coughed vigorously the moment he took the drags in.

I could see that he wasn't able to handle the hit, his eyes rolled and cockeyed and he kept trying hard to sit straight.

The girl next to him pushed him further on the couch and climbed over him.

Half the people sitting around had their eyes on them.

The girl got some spirit in a glass and repeatedly passed it into the guy's mouth from her's.

Just when I thought I'd get up from the couch, the girl came close to guy's ears and asked him in a whisper that was loud enough for me to hear clearly, 'Your place or mine?'

What the guy did next shocked me and everyone around,

he wobbled some loud words and pushed the girl so hard off him that she hit the ground with a thud.

With alcohol spilled on his shirt and all eyes on him, he left the party amid loud cries of the girl.

Now, let me make one more thing clear, infact very clear, by now I've learnt a lot about Indian men, and that day when I saw a half sober Indian male violently rejecting open invitation for sex, it had me thinking.

In my last look at him, as he exited the party almost toppling over at the exit and trying hard to keep himself balanced. I noticed a strange smile on his face and a craving in his eyes that I never forgot.

Right now, as I sit in this big group of my Italian friends in this apartment at a high rise, I pass my joint to the guy sitting next to me and funny that life is, I realise it's him.

The craving in the eyes is the same, and it drives me to ask him, "So what's your name?"

"A, uh, a, Ali... My name's Ali." he said, stuttering at every word of it.

6

COMING BACK TO LIFE

"I'm Christa." She said, almost taken aback by my sudden stuttering and the blank expression on my face.

I couldn't recall what happened later that night, but we talked, I remember our voices in the noisy room, and I remember I talked far more than I'd talked to anybody in the past few months.

Hash and beautiful women do that to you, you'd normally go mute and weak in the knees seeing them, but when you're high, and deprived of company, you open up, and I did open up that night.

I remember talking more than she replied to me, and I was afraid if I'd gone way too honest and blunt with her, because that'd mean asking her out the moment she turned towards me, but I couldn't remember any of it the next morning when I woke up, I just remember that we talked.

I woke up in the morning and found myself sleeping on the floor rug, the same place where I'd sat with Sandy last night.

Sandy was also asleep where he had been sitting and so were the few of the people who'd come last night, all of them passed out.

It was six in the morning and a Saturday, so I'd no office.

I stood up and made my way through all the people sleeping randomly on the floor.

I strolled to my room and there was someone in my bed, I went close by and checked, it was the girl from last night. Christa, I recalled her name after stressing my mind for more than a minute.

She was snoring hard, with her mouth open.

It was difficult for me to not to fall in love with her at that very instant, and it's a terrible feeling to have, because you tend to disgust yourself for falling for someone whose name you try hard to recall, and with whom you've had just one conversation, which you can't recall at all.

I made coffee for myself and went to the balcony for a smoke.

After a while, someone called out from behind, "That's Ali, right?" I knew the voice, it was her.

"Oh, hi Christa" I said suddenly turning around, hating myself for my paced heartbeat and trying hard to talk smooth and easy.

"Is that coffee? Can I have some?" she said rubbing her eyes and adjusting to the sunlight.

"Oh yeah, sure" I said offering her my mug. "Oh no, I mean I'll get you some" I said and made my way to the kitchen. I wish it was possible to kick yourself in the ass.

"I wanna go out somewhere today. Can you give me some company?" she said as I got coffee for her.

"What?!" I blurted as she suddenly looked at me startled, "no I mean sure. Yeah sure" I said and left the balcony, getting a strong urge to stab myself in the chest.

✿✿

I called up Balu and asked him for his car.

I didn't know where we were going or where Christa wanted to go, and didn't bother asking her.

We first went to her flat as she had asked me to, saying she needed to change and pick up something.

It was in a far off corner of the city, which she said was a small township full of non Indians.

It was early morning on a weekend so roads were mostly empty, and we'd left the house while all others were still sleeping.

I tried talking to Christa to ask her about what she did and what had bought her here, because she sure didn't look like a hippie.

I started with Holika and how she knew her, she told me she doesn't know Holika, and had come with another friend of hers who knew Holika.

I tried other ways of asking her many things, but she answered short and crisp and mostly just looked out of the window as I drove.

On a long stretch of road, surrounded by the country side and leading to the other side of the city, I took a look at her as she calmly looked out of the window.

I didn't know what this girl wanted, or why I was driving her to her house, but her fair skin and black hair were like a concoction, one which could easily honey trap any normal man. And I ridiculed myself for being no different.

Add to that her welling black eyes and an Italianised English accent, she had an élan that could get you into ruins, a crazy, wild elegance which would mute glib talkers.

She would make you speak everything, but knew the art of exuding that she won't open up to you, and you'd accept the fact, but will never stop trying.

In a few hours I spent with her, I realised she can make you feel important to her, and then make you feel invisible, and it all happens before you catch it, and by the time you do, you find yourself helpless.

We arrived at the place, the wide highway led to many interlinked narrow alleys, one of which had her building.

The area mostly had foreigners roaming the streets, with few Indian shops and vendors.

As Christa got down, there was a wide smile on her face and most of the people around her building seemed to indentify her.

She waved at and talked to many of them, which made me believe she was not at her house since few days.

"Ali, are you coming upstairs?" She said as I looked at her old building with many balconies, most of which had foreigners standing and chatting.

"Yes, sure" I said and we walked in.

"Miss Christa!" I heard a loud voice from the top floor as we climbed he weary staircase that led to her house.

I looked up to find an old, paunchy Indian man in a vest looking angrily at her, "Don't look up, just walk!" she said pulling me from my hand.

Before I could react, the man shouted again, looking down from the top floor, "Miss Christa! Please listen to me!"

"Oh damn!" she whispered looking at me and then looked up at the man, "Just two more days Sir, you get it when I get it." She said smiling at him.

"But that's what you said two weeks ago. And after that you just disappeared" he shouted back, relatively calm this time, while I looked at both of them clueless.

"Sir, l am really sorry, but I'd lost my key." She said smiling at him. "and now no more wait, just give me another two three days" she said and opened the door of her house.

I stood there looking at the old man while he looked back at me in frowning in anger, "Come in, don't look at him, otherwise he'll come down and shout" she said pulling me inside by the hand.

"But who was he?" I asked puzzled.

"My landlord, very greedy man, just three months rent due and he's already going mad" she said and winked.

"Well this is a, uh, nice little place you've got here." I said looking around her apartment.

I'd been to many bachelor pads where people stay alone and throw things around.

But I'd never seen anything quite like this. The mess in her living room was so rigid, and so uniformly spread, that it almost looked like it had been organizing itself this way since years.

"I've been here for about three months," she said, "and yeah I know, it's pretty messy"

Her landline phone rung just as she said that, and we both started looking around to spot the instrument dug in the deep mess.

She climbed over one of the cartons filled with old books and almost toppled over it to pull out a suitcase from underneath it.

"I stuck it in the suitcase, to muffle the sound." She said looking at me as she opened the old suitcase to take out the telephone from inside.

She talked on the phone hysterically, whispering many Italian words to herself which sure sounded like swear words.

"I'll change and come. We have to rush!" she said and went to the other room shutting the door behind her.

By the time I found a corner to sit, which was actually some more mess piled up high enough to be used as a seat, she came back from the room.

She wore a large black hat with black glasses, over a knee length black dress.

The smell of her perfume filled the room, and I think, looking at her that very moment, I'd have taken an hour to react if she wouldn't have spoken something.

"Shall we go, Ali" she asked, stressing on my name, which clearly meant she'd caught me gaping.

"Yeah, sure" I said, again with the stab-myself-in-the-chest feeling.

Just as we walked out, there was a large cat sitting in front of her door and before I could react, it pounced on me and straightaway crawled and sat on my shoulders.

"Whoa! What's that?" I exclaimed, trying to tackle it.

"Oh you're scaring it" she said running her hand over it while it tried to sit on my shoulders.

"Uh, is it yours? Well uh, I'm... Sorry" I said wondering if it was normal to open a door and be pounced upon by a large cat heads on, because she made it look that way.

"Is he alright?" I asked running my hand over its fur and trying to hold it to put it down on the floor.

"Sure. He's okay, aren't you, Cat?" She said patting her on its head, "And it won't come down now, until you carry it till the ground floor. Poor old cat, that's how he is. He climbs up on anyone's shoulders and doesn't come down until you walk down till the ground floor, isn't it Cat?"

"Uh well, Ok." I said as we started walking down the stairs, with the cat almost comfortably fitting onto my shoulders now.

"What's his name by the way?" I asked midway down the stairs.

"I don't know his name and l don't have the right to give him one. So I call it Cat, that's what they call it in English right? I don't own him, neither does he, we just met one day, and we stay together." She said, with me looking at her almost dumbfounded, by the sheer weirdness of her thoughts and the optimism with which they came out.

I thought my expression had embarrassed her, but to my surprise she continued, "I don't own anything, and l won't own anything, until l find a place where me and things go together. I'm not sure where that is, but l know what it's like. It's like Jewels." She completed and looked at me smiling, tangling me in the complexity and randomness of her talk.

"Okay. So by Jewels, do you by any chance, mean The Jewels, that high-end jewellery store in the city?" I asked, trying to find something sane to reply.

"Bingo! The Jewels, the jewellery store near, uh, I forgot the name of that road."

"Brigades" I said.

We reached down and the cat instantly slipped off my shoulders just as I came out of the building.

"Yes, the Brigades. I'm crazy about The Jewels." She said and took the car keys from my hand as we reached the car.

"Listen" I tried to interrupt her but she walked to the driver's side and signalled me to sit on the other side.

"See Christa, do you know driving?" I asked as she sat in the driver's seat. She continued talking completely ignoring my question and started the car. I frantically hopped in the other seat.

"So yeah, The Jewels," she said and accelerated the car with a jerk, oblivious to the panic on my face and making it impossible for me to interrupt her, "You know those days, when you get the mean reds?" she said, now driving fairly well for the jerky start.

I didn't know whether to ask her about letting me drive or join her completely out of context conversation, "The mean reds? What's that?" I asked, accepting the fact that I didn't have a choice now.

"The reds, the mean reds! C'mon, don't you get the reds sometimes?" she asked as we joined the highway.

I thought hard to myself and tried to relate her Italianized English vocabulary to anything that it remotely matched with, "by any chance, do you mean the blues? As in getting the blues?" I asked hoping this was going somewhere, and so was the car.

"No. The blues are when you're fat or if it's raining, that's all. But the reds, reds are horrible, that's why I call them mean reds. Suddenly you're afraid and don't know what of. You just want to run away from it all. Do you ever get that feeling?"

"Well, uh, yeah, I sure do" that is all I could reply with.

But she continued, "When I get it, all that does any good is to jump in a cab and go to The Jewels. Calms me down right away. The quietness and grandness of it. Nothing bad could happen there. If I could find a real place that made me feel like Jewels, then I'd buy some furniture and give the cat a name."

The Jewels was a jewellery showroom full of expensive diamonds and platinum, and was built with a façade of domes and small minaret's to give it a royal look.

Last I heard, people who went there to shop would have run out of places to stash their money, and when you're busy evading your landlord for three months of unpaid rent, The Jewels was surely a place that would throw you into meaner reds.

"So you go to The Jewels when you're down, that's a pretty expensive affair huh" I said trying to get her to say who paid the bills for her therapy diamonds.

"No. Not at all. The air there is free. I just stroll in the galleria, and sometimes get a pie and a coffee from the shop nearby. It's pretty good, you should try it"

"Oh, alright" I said blankly looking at her.

I noticed we'd driven further towards the countryside of the city. In all the chaotic flow of her ideas, most of which were making it difficult for me to find words to reply or even an appropriate reaction, I hadn't paid attention to the way, and we were now totally out of the city, into the vast green farms with no sign of buildings around.

"Whoa! Where are we?" I asked startled by the view.

"Ah, nice country side isn't it" she said looking around, "I've absolutely no idea where this car is taking us"

"What?! Seriously?!" I exclaimed, but she kept driving down the highway, and in reply just looked at me lowering her sunglasses and smiled.

I let out a sigh, tried to sound a little serious and turned towards her, "See Christa, all the talking that you're doing, it's good. But we're miles away from the city now, and you're just driving down this highway without any sense of direction. This is not a place to hang out, believe me, there's nothing to come for miles ahead and..."

"There is, and will you do something for me?" she asked cutting me short.

"Pick up that black folder from the back seat and open it" she said before I could reply.

I reluctantly turned backwards and picked up the folder, it was stuffed with papers, most of them letterheads with some strange text and some English printed over them.

"What is all this?" I asked picking up one of the papers.

"Don't touch them, it took me hours to arrange them" she said and suddenly turned the car to a dusty, narrow lane joining the highway, "take this, and pin it to your shirt" she stretched her hand to the folder and pulled out a small ID card with a clip.

It read 'Ambasciata d'Italia' in big bold letters, with an emblem which had a star, stamped with the words 'Diplomat'. "What is this?" I asked her puzzled.

"Look where we're heading darling. We're home!" she said smiling at me.

I looked to the end of the dusty road where she'd taken the car, there were massive iron gates and a very high compound wall sprawling from its sides. The semicircular board on the top of the gates read, "Bengaluru Central Prison"

I was dumbfounded.

"What the heck is this?!" I said after a moment of numbness and felt my senses going into a panic.

The car had driven into the zone surrounded with barbed wires and gunmen manned gun towers.

Suddenly I got a feeling that I'd gone too far today with this unknown Italian girl, I started getting ideas of her duping me into the prison with all the sweet talk that she did on the way, I'd read somewhere that Indian police locks up random men from the road to let go the felons inside the prison, so that the headcount of the prison is unaffected.

In those few seconds as our car reached the parking bay, which was filled with police jeeps, I realized I was blankly looking at her as she was driving, imagining myself hung naked upside down in a dark prison cell.

"Okay. Who are you? And why have you got me here?" I managed to speak with a shiver as she braked the car in the parking.

"Oh my God! Look at your face! I should ask you who you are, 'cause you don't look the same anymore!" she said laughing and removed her glasses.

"This is a prison for God's sake, why the hell have we come here?" I asked again, as she bent to the back seat to pick up the black folder and pulled out a similar ID card from it.

"Don't freak out you weak Indian! Pin up that ID card and we're good to go." She said pinning the ID card on her lapel and wore her black hat and glasses as she stepped out of the car.

"Good to go where?" I asked getting out of the car and pinned the ID card same way as her.

"Inside the jails, this is my workplace" she said and strode forward.

"What? We've to go inside?" I said following her and realised we were already at the checking unit.

Around dozen prison guards with guns lazed around in the area, couple of them came forward to frisk me.

After a light frisking and a close look at my ID card, they let me in.

They seemed to recognize Christa, and she seemed way too familiar with the place, the guards looked at her and chuckled amongst themselves as the female guards frisked her.

She whispered something to herself that sounded like some Italian slur.

"Okay, so why are we here. And you better be clear now, 'cos this is not funny" I asked her just as we got cleared of the checking and entered a narrow, dark lobby.

"You saw how those bastards were gaping, everyone does that here. That's why I got you along. Don't worry, we'll leave soon" she said walking forward.

"But why on earth we have come here in the first place?" I asked and then unknowingly my voice turned into a loud shout that resonated in the empty hall we were walking across, "What the fuck Christa! Would you now tell me what the heck is happening here and what are you upto?"

She looked at me in a serious expression for a moment and said, "Okay listen. On December 31st 2009, twelve Italian men and women, precisely six men and six women, arrived at Delhi airport with a tourist visa, and with cocaine. Since then they're rotting here, and I'm rotting in India. I don't know whether they're guilty or not, and now I don't even care, but I was sent from the government of Italy to get them extradited, which I don't think would happen anytime soon in your Indian courts. So now all I do is visit this bunch of bastards every few days and report back to the Italian embassy that they're alive here. This is my job, they pay me in peanuts, and I'll be declared disloyal to my government if I leave an assignment midway. So I'm stuck in this mess and it's already been a year like this. I'm sorry to have got you here, 'cos you really don't need to do this, but I woke up in the morning and I'd to come here today. You were the only one awake, and if I'd have told you where we were headed you would never have come. Do this favour of accompanying me here for sometime today, will you?"

"You both, get inside" A policeman came and interrupted before I could say anything.

He was a usual fat Indian policeman and did his usual gaping.

There was anger and frustration on Christa's face, and I knew I was a partial reason behind it.

I tried to sync in all that she had said while he led us through the lobby. We had to stoop down to cross a small passage with iron doors that led us to a wide illuminated room with many policeman guarding an entrance.

There was a queue of visitors at the prison, Christa and I joined it, waiting for each person to be thoroughly frisked by the guards before the entrance.

Christa still wore her large hat and glasses and looked disgusted of the place.

More than half the policemen sitting by the walls were not taking their eyes off her, and she looked familiar of it.

It was hard to believe that a girl like her, beautiful and elegant and from whom I had heard only pleasant things till now, would be dealing with such rash and morbid place day in and day out.

No wonder she talked about meaner reds than the blues, and the clean air of The Jewels were medicine to her.

Looking at her, I thought to myself that it was hard for someone to stay so calm and mostly smiling, when unwillingly stuck in a foreign country for over a year and have a job that gets you nothing more than a menacing landlord and the mean reds.

We reached the gate, and were frisked and let in.

Around hundreds of people sat in a huge hall, almost all of them handcuffed, and I noticed the room had absolutely no ventilation.

The iron door behind us was closed every time someone was let in, and another door on the other end was permanently closed. It was the meeting room of the prison.

There were murmurs, loud cries, and sharp stench of sweat and alcohol which couldn't escape out and had rigged the hall.

Again, Christa seemed familiar of it all and straightaway walked to the last row of the seat arrangement.

I followed her through the overcrowded mess of people randomly sitting on the floor.

The last row had Christa's people, all twelve of them, they sat in a row and looked almost wasted.

The men were terribly unkempt with dense beards and expressionless faces, and the women seemed pitiful. But, strangely enough, they all seemed settled into the prison, and in a way acknowledged the chaos and rigidness of the place through their laid back demeanour.

Christa went to each one of them and made them sign on a sheet of paper, which was to record their presence there.

Few of them said something to her which she noted down.

She then took out an official letter with Italian text and read it aloud to all of them.

My mind was reeling under the smell and sordidness of the place.

She quietly finished her tasks and we walked out in the open without speaking a word. Coming out in the open, just after a few minutes in the prison air, gave me a strong sense of freedom and what it could mean.

There was just a wall separating freedom and foundation of one's life, and I could feel what it meant by just looking into the open green fields.

We sat in the car and I drove back to the highway.

Christa quietly sat looking out of the window and lit a cigarette. "See, uh, Christa, I'm sorry if I sounded rude there. I didn't know that was your job" I said trying to check if she was fine.

"You know nothing about me darling" she said smirking at me.

I came home late in the evening, dropping Christa at the Jewels. We did the usual goodbyes and she asked me to leave, saying she wanted to be alone there.

Holika sat on the couch reading one of the books I'd given her when I entered. The people from last night were gone, and the house was cleaned up.

"Where were you?" Holika asked noticing me enter.

"Office" I said and went to my room.

Collapsing on my bed, images of Christa throbbed in my head.

I tried to tell myself that she'd just asked me for a drop, and it meant nothing more, hoping to convince myself on the latter.

I still couldn't recall what we had started talking last night, but remembered her face when she'd turned towards me asking me my name and had got me dumbfounded.

It was hard to read her mind and keep her out of your mind. I found that terrible, but ignoring her and not finding myself thinking about her repeatedly was a difficult thing to do.

Maybe she already had someone in her life, but she had a persona that would make it tough for someone not to fall for her.

Maybe all the thoughts about her spiralling up and down my mind were triggered solely by my loneliness and quest for company, and our meeting meant nothing for a day in her life, or maybe, just maybe, even she might be going to bed with me in her mind.

"Where were you?" Sandy asked entering the room and broke my chain of thoughts.

"Office" I replied and pulled the blanket over my head.

"Fuck you!" I could hear him respond.

7

THE REDS

"You look better nowadays, looks like you're recovering." Michael told me few days later in office.

"Maybe, just been amongst few friends lately, so life's getting better"

It'd been three days since my prison visit with Christa, and I regretted not asking her her number that day, because I doubted if she'll try to get in touch with me again, and dropping by her little chaotic place just to say hi seemed out of option.

I went back to my house that day and as usual, worked out and watched TV.

My schedule had been the same for months now, and I'd almost started to fit into it.

Though I'd accepted the fact that meeting Christa meant nothing that day, everything about our meeting nagged me into thinking that it wasn't over, and the look in her eyes that day kept hovering around in my thoughts.

I hesitated to go to her house and meet her, because I didn't had any significant reason to tell her why I drove all the way till there.

I'd asked Holika a few times about her, but each time it couldn't go beyond my desperate efforts to make her recall who from the big party that night I was asking about.

"Ali, someone came asking for you" Holika said just as I returned from the gym with Sandy.

"Who?"

"She left her number" she said and gave me a small note.

It had a phone number and *'Christa'* written under it.

"Oh! Christa." Sandy said reading the chit from behind.

"What? You know her?" I asked.

"No, but you know her!" he said trying an idiotic, excited face.

"Fuck off!" I said and dialled the number.

"Hey Christa, Ali this side" I said on hearing her voice on the other side.

"Ali? Who Ali?" she snapped back immediately.

I was shocked and didn't know what to say.

"Chill, kidding" she said and continued without a pause, "Can you come to my house?"

"When?"

"ASAP"

"ASAP as in now?"

"Your take, Mr. Whats-your-name" she said and disconnected.

I looked at the time, it was eight into the night. I called up Balu and picked up his car from the office parking.

I reached her township in around an hour, it was a different place at night, with bright lighting and streets crowded with foreigners.

Her building entrance too had many young foreigners chatting in groups, I climbed the stairs to reach her apartment.

The main door was ajar, and through the opening I could see a crowd of people inside.

I entered to find a small boisterous party going on inside.

It was surprising to see some ten twelve people stuffed in that smoke filled room, with the enormous mess still unmoved.

Christa sat in one corner of the hall, chatting with a female friend. I noticed I'd seen her in my apartment the day Christa had come.

"Hey, Ali!" Christa called out seeing me standing at the door.

"Hi" I said looking around and finding no Indian in the crowd.

Christa looked sloshed out, with red eyes and a constant smile on her face.

"Meet my friend Ann, she's throwing a party" she said and I smiled at Ann, who was visibly far more sloshed than Christa.

"Come, I'll get you a drink" she said pulling me by the hand towards her kitchen which now looked like a mini bar.

"I'm fine. I'll make myself a mocktail. I don't drink now" I said searching for a softdrink bottles amongst all the alcohol.

"Why?" she asked, taking support from my shoulder to stand erect.

"Bad experience with it" I said, remembering Michael's party.

"Or call it once bitten twice shy" she said winking at me.

"What?" I asked, shocked by her reply.

"Never mind, get yourself a Coke atleast" she said and moved towards the crowd, leaving me thinking about her reply.

After sometime, Christa asked me to go on a walk with her, leaving the people in her house still partying.

She changed her party clothes and dressed up in pyjamas and tshirt, and I know she caught me gaping.

We came down the stairs, without getting noticed by the loud group inside.

"We'll walk this way" Christa said just as we got to the street.

The other side of the street was a dimly lit, calmer part of the stretch.

We walked, and I tried hard to keep my glances away from her face which shone under the moonlight, and with no makeup and her hair scattering on her face, it was hard to do so.

After a moment of silence, she spoke, "So that day you got to know what I do, now tell me, what do you do?"

"I write stories, but for a living, I write computer codes" I said.

"Stories? What kind of stories?"

"Incomplete stories, I start writing them but abandon them midway." I said. And that was probably the first time I told anyone that I write anything other than computer codes.

"Why do you abandon them?" she asked.

"I have to, because they never get completed. I've a lot of stories, but all of them incomplete"

"You want a story?" she asked.

"Yes, but a one that completes" I said and noticed we'd reached the other end of the street.

We walked up and down the street till late into the night, and remained silent for more time than we talked.

It was midnight when everyone in her apartment except Ann had left, she sighed with relief and decided to go home.

I came till her door to see her off, and after a moment of silence, we kissed.

I didn't know how it happened, and who came forward first, but while we were at it, I felt almost lost into myself.

I closed my eyes and we kissed passionately, waiting for the other person to let go first. After almost a minute, she slipped out her lips from mine.

"It's late. You must go now." she said taking her hands off me.

"Bye" I said and silently went down the stairs, holding myself from the embarrassment of looking back at her face.

Days went by and the first sudden kiss between me and Christa transformed into many later.

Almost everyday I drove to her apartment after office and chatted for long hours with her and Ann, who was her roommate now.

They told me about Delhi and their days at Paharganj, their meeting with people like Fred and the case Christa was stuck in.

Whenever we got sometime off to ourselves, we roamed the streets and she clicked pictures.

I showed her Hindi movies and she laughed through most of them, even when whole of theatre was silent. Sometimes, she cried too.

She gave me Italian movie CD's, I never put one on in my laptop, but always told her I watched them.

All this while I realised one thing, roaming on busy Indian streets with a white skinned foreigner woman next to you is an experience in itself.

The look on people's face sometimes told me that they're mistaking me for Christa's guide, but mostly they just gaped at her, and wondered how a guy like me had managed something like her, I too wondered the same.

Christa had her way with Indian vendors and shopkeepers, through her sweet talks and their fixation for foreigners.

Almost always she had a far better sense of dressing up then me, and told me that shabby clothes for foreigners worked in Delhi, not in Bangalore.

I started feeling the brightness and newness in my life, the last few months that I'd lived parched in addiction and heartbreak had begun to fade away.

One evening Christa and I were strolling at the galleria of The Jewels, with the regular pie and coffee in her hands.

I usually accompanied Christa to The Jewels, and all we did there was just strolling down the galleria, sometimes holding hands.

It was late in the night and the security guard asked us to move out, with us being almost the last ones remaining in the lobby.

There was heavy rain outside, and we had to wait at the porch of the Jewels for the downpour to slow down.

After few minutes of waiting, when The Jewels' officials locked up the showroom and left with their umbrellas, we found ourselves standing there alone in the night.

"There's a shortcut to the parking, we've to go to the street on the backside, sticking through the sides of this building" Christa said.

"What? Why do we go to that street? The car parking is in the other direction" I exclaimed.

"No! There is a shortcut. Through the basement of this building." She said and started walking.

"Basement of this building?" I asked her puzzled.

"Yes, the entrance to it is through the street on the backside" she said and pulled me by the hand.

We walked struggling to save ourselves from the rain through the small shade surrounding the walls of the building.

"Where's the entrance?" I said as we reached the narrow street, my shoes were drenched in the puddles and the rain was getting heavier.

"There you go!" she shouted and pushed me hard into a big water puddle. I slipped and fell flat into it, wetting myself from top to bottom.

"What the fuck Christa!" I said and got up struggling.

Just as I wiped the mud and water off my face, she pounced over me and pushed me to the wall on the opposite side of the street.

Before I could figure it out, we were kissing each other to the extent of almost biting each other's lips. She clung her body as much as she could against mine, and let the pouring rain drench us both.

The rain was wild and the feeling of her wet skin under my palms shifted me into a strange trance, we kissed passionately and wildly. Blame it on the rain, the moment, or the suppleness of her skin, for the first time I let my hands fumble over her body.

Under the heavy rain, I slipped my hands to her bare waist and further up her shirt, she seethed and kissed without stopping. I unpinned her brassieres and slipped my hands over her breasts.

Maybe the age old psychology of rain does that to Indian men, but I lost myself into her and forgot we were on the street. I unbuttoned her trousers and let my hands slowly slip into them.

"We're on the street Ali" she suddenly whispered in my ear and I snapped back into the moment.

With both of us completely drenched under the heavy rain, I carried her in my arms through the empty road and walked to the car.

The car was parked in a mesh of many cars and there was absolutely no lighting in the parking.

I dropped her on the back seat and as soon as we both were in, the passion surpassed the space issues and we both started undressing each other.

I turned the heater on full blown. In the stark darkness, growing heat in the car and with our bodies melting into each other, I don't know what happened, but Christa stopped me and retracted.

"Oh shit, what are we doing?" she said snapping back and looked at me blankly.

"Drive me home Ali, will you?" she said fumbling around for her clothes.

I noticed sweat beads and embarrassment on her face. She wore back her brassieres and put on the shirt lying next to her, which was mine.

I drove shirtless till her apartment, and we didn't speak anything throughout the journey.

I got up in the morning on the couch in Christa's house, half naked and in the same pants as last night.

On the window I noticed my wet shirt from last night drying up, which she had wore back to the house.

The room was empty and there seemed no sign of Christa is the house.

She had left me a text that she was going to some office with Ann, I made coffee in her kitchen, looked out from the balcony and lit a cigarette.

Flashes of last night's crazy rain, the street, and the backseat of Balu's car flashed in my mind.

I thought of Christa's shocked and perturbed face when she came back to the moment, I now remember how we were repeatedly trying to rearrange ourselves in the confined backseat of the car.

It all looked stupid and embarrassing to me now, and I guessed that's why Christa had gone out without informing me, to save ourselves from having to look at each other.

I stepped out putting my shirt back, and as usual the Cat came and settled over my shoulder.

I cuddled and played with its fur a little, and dropped him to the street.

'Left keys in the letterbox. Let's meet in the evening.' I sent her a text and drove down the long highway, with the lush country side greens overpowering my hidden mean-reds.

✿✿

Christa called me after a couple of days, and asked me to come home.

I didn't try to call her since past two days, except a few text messages. It was strange on her side, but I thought of letting her take her time and waited for her to call back, which she finally did.

I called Balu and after urging him to do some alterations in his schedule, he let me pick up the car from office parking.

I reached Christa's place in the evening, and noticed she had considerably cleaned up the mess.

She came from her room and smiled at me, the warmth in her smile was new, one that I hadn't seen before.

She came forward and hugged me and gave me a slight kiss. Her sleepy black eyes and no makeup on her face reflected her sedative, tranquilizing beauty.

"What's the matter?" I asked as she walked to the kitchen to get coffee for me.

"Nothing" she said handling me the coffee mug and threw her arms around my shoulders.

I looked into her black, drowsy eyes. A peaceful and relaxed smile rested on her face. It was a high that couldn't be sold in bottles or packets.

"I called you to stay" she whispered passively.

"Stay where?" I asked.

"Right here. With me." she whispered coming close to my ear and rested her head on my shoulder.

Days went by and I started spending most of my time at Christa's place. Half of my wardrobe from my flat was now mixed into Christa's. Sometimes I stayed over and went to office directly from her place. Our bond grew stronger than

I had ever imagined. At times, I used to remind myself about why she was here in India. Though she no longer seemed that annoyed of India anymore, as she had swiftly settled by now. There was always a thought hovering in my mind that her stay will sooner or later hit a dead-end.

I never really gathered the courage to clearly ask her when her case would be resolving and when she would have to return. My senses told me thinking of this relationship as an eternal, everlasting one was foolish. But still I could never bring myself to be completely convinced upon that. I always knew we were heading somewhere with this.

But I never ever had the slightest of idea that we would end up, the way we ended up. Or the way I ended up, and the way she ended up.

8

FROM HERE...

The ringtone of my phone shook me up from dead sleep. It was dark and only light in the room was from the ringing cellphone. I reached out for the phone and squinted at the screen. It was Christa.

"Wake up!" she said as soon as I answered.

"What happened?" I grumbled.

"Ali. Get up. We need to go somewhere!" she said on the other side almost shouting into the mouthpiece.

"Go where?" I asked.

"You first get the car and come to my apartment. Now!"

"Now? It's four in the morning Christa. I have office tomorrow. Where do you wanna go?" I asked checking out the time and noticing it was still dark outside.

"Will you come if I tell you where?" she asked.

"I will not come even if you tell me. Now go back to sleep and let me also sleep. I will come there in the evening after office." I said

"Ali. Pick up that damn car and come. If you come in evening, I don't think you'll find anyone here. I'm serious. So get up and come." she said and disconnected.

I took a moment to register what she had said before disconnecting. 'Was Christa leaving India?' I thought to myself and a shiver ran through me.

With confusion and panic inside my head, I hurriedly grabbed the car keys and ran out to the elevator.

I took wrong lanes, drove down muddy shortcuts and sped as hard as I could to reach Christa's place in half an hour.

Braking the car with a screech, I ran up the staircase of her building and slammed open the door of her house.

Christa sat on the slab of her kitchen in her nightsuit. Ann stood next to her. And though the mess in her living room appeared to be stacked away into a corner all at once, the house in no way looked like she was going to leave.

"Whoa! How did you come so early?" she asked startled and got down from the kitchen slab.

"It was a joke. Right?" I asked in a plain, serious tone.

She paused for a moment and said, "No. It wasn't. You really wouldn't have found me here if you had come in the evening"

"Why? Where are you going?" I asked.

"Not just me. We both are going." she said coming close to me and threw her arms around me.

"But where? What's happening Christa. Tell me clearly" I asked. It was hard not to kiss her forehead and brush off the strands of hair falling over her face.

"It's like that day Ali, if I would tell you where we are going, you would create a ruckus and won't come. If I would have told you the place that day too, you would never have come, right?"

"I'll come, but you gotta tell me the place."

"It's 300 kilometers away"

"What?"

"We're going by car."

"What?"

"To Pondicherry."

"What?"

"We're going to Pondicherry. 300 kilometres from here. You, me and Ann, in your car."

"What?!"

"Stop these whats and speak something! Yes! We're going!"

"No way in the hell Christa! 300 kilometres?! Wow! You've gone crazy!"

"Ali, you see that backpack? It's mine, I've already packed up, and we're going" she said in a serious tone.

"You can't be serious! Why the hell you wanna go so far right now?!" I asked.

"'Cause Pondicherry has beaches, sands, and Fred"

"What?!"

"Yes, remember I told you about Fred? He's come down to Pondicherry for two days, and so Ann and I want to meet him. You too want to meet him Ali!"

"No I don't" I said

"Yes you do! Two days is all I'm asking from you, darling" she said and smiled at me mockingly.

"This is not funny Christa" I said.

"Definitely not" she said and again clung onto me, "We should hit the road very soon. So call up your idiotic driver friend and make up some story" she pecked my cheek and went into the room to arrange her stuff.

I sighed and called up Balu. He had woken up to my call and his freaking out lasted for almost a minute.

His work with the car seemed far more important than driving down 300 kilometres to meet some random person whom I had no intentions of meeting. He said he'd have to cancel his airport pickups and till the last minute I disconnected the call, kept on asking me if I was serious.

I dropped a mail to Michael, saying I would be back in couple of days. I had a pile up of vacation days available to me, so office wasn't a problem.

I wondered was there a specific reason behind what Christa portrayed as a sudden whim to drive to Pondicherry. Her need to meet Fred seemed imperative rather than unplanned and casual. I could see the urgency in her eyes. But then I looked at Christa again as she chatted with Ann in the kitchen. She was laughing her heart out at something, to the extent of almost welling her eyes up. I decided I would go.

I packed in a few of my clothes from her apartment and we left for Pondicherry.

The road to Pondicherry was a broad highway with less traffic, and we covered 300 kilometres in around four hours of non stop driving.

Fred had arranged a beach facing cottage away from the main city. We reached around an hour after the sunrise. Ann and Christa had slept through most of the way. I too snoozed a few times while driving; waking up to the trailers overtaking me.

We reached an open area near the beach which had a few temporary shacks and cottages erected in a row.

A guy came walking towards us, shouting out something in heavily Americanised English.

"That's Fred" Christa told me while Ann walked towards him.

Fred was an unruly, bulky American who could rough up most Indian men without a second thought.

His handshake was a clenching one and he had a wild air about himself. His curly locks fell on the sides of his face and it looked like his shoulders overshadowed all of us.

He led us to the cottage that we four had to share. There were four beds put in the room in plain symmetry. I was tired from the driving, and thought of hitting the bed instantly.

"Hey brother, what are you doing? See what I got." Fred called out to me seeing me go to bed. He flashed a small packet towards me which had some white powder, probably cocaine.

"Grade A coke buddy, you don't get it easily" he said.

I sat up on my bed and looked at him cleanly arranging a streak of the white powder with a plastic card.

"There you go man. Snort it" he said signalling towards the cleanly arranged powder stripes.

I mulled for a moment and replied, "Thanks but I don't snort. Sorry. You do it". I'd never snorted any powder up my nose. I'd read stories where people snorted, bled from their nose and never rose up.

Ann and Fred snorted two clean streaks of the powder and it hit them instantly. Fred managed to lie on the bed while Ann went flat out on the floor itself.

I lay down on my bed and Christa came next to me and hugged me tightly. I thought of asking her why she had suddenly come here but noticed her already dozed off. I kissed her forehead and went to sleep.

✿✿

We woke up in the afternoon went out to laze around at the beach. It was after months that I'd seen a horizon which wasn't made of buildings or concrete. We had a heavy meal, smoked hash, and sat on the beach for hours with the sea waves hitting our feet.

Christa sat next to me resting her head on my shoulder and holding my hand. We sat quietly for hours, with our eyes fixed at the recurring waves and our minds stoned and tranquilized by the strong hash.

In my calmed and zoned out head, I could clearly feel the awkwardness that the whole air of this journey had since the moment I reached Christa's home in the morning and we left. There was restlessness in her eyes each time I looked at her since leaving for the journey. She pretended to be calm and composed, and it wasn't working one bit.

Christa and I asked Fred and Ann to stroll about in the city, but they insisted upon staying in the cottage, probably to snort some more.

It was difficult to say that they were together, one could easily call them lovers, but I guess they were somewhere at the thin line that was hard to define. It was evident that they both wanted to live nomadic and free lives, free from any vow or promise whatsoever.

They did want to be together, but not at the cost of compromising their freedom, and when you leave your country and past behind for a moment of that freedom, you ironically get bounded by it and grow too protective of it.

Christa and I rented a bike from the cottage and left to wander in the city.

Under the hot afternoon sun, we walked along the beaches on the way, ate local sea food, and rode the bike through windy highways. The locals guided us to war memorials and churches. I stood outside one of the churches while Christa spent around half an hour inside.

She came out with red and swollen eyes and smiled on seeing me noticing her, "Don't worry. It's nothing. God does that to me." She said smiling.

We reached the cottage late in the night, at about eleven. Fred and Ann sat in the room, with Fred flicking channels on TV and Ann lying passed out on his lap.

Christa and I had our dinner from the cottage mess and came out in the open. She snuggled in my arms and we quietly walked down the beach.

Our feet dug in the wet sand with each step and the roar of the sea in the dark soothed our ears.

We kept on walking for long and reached the far end of the beach. It was past midnight and there was no one around. Grainy moonlight filled the eerie darkness and the starts brightly dotted the dark sky.

The rapid wind blew Christa's hair on my face repeatedly. We sat at a spot next to many empty boats parked in a row. Christa snuggled into my arms and started reminding me of all our days together. She clearly remembered each time we had met, even the minutest of our meetings. To hear her speak all that was unsettling and comforting at the same time. She gave me more thoughts to mull over her demeanour that day.

She kept speaking in a strange monotony, with her voice breaking up a few times and her eyes getting teary. Just before she was about to talk about the car incident, she came forward, looked at me blankly for a moment, and kissed me.

She pushed me to the sand and stretched herself over me, kissing me while the waves drenched us. I kissed her back and in the cool breeze and the roar of the sea, I got lost into her yet again.

Our hands wandered over our wet bodies yet again, reminding us of the night in the car.

Kissing passionately and gradually forgetting the open skies, we stripped each other down, and unhurriedly and softly, made love right there on the beach.

"I love you" she whispered in my ear after a while when we lay naked on the beach facing the starry sky with the waves hitting our bodies.

Surprisingly, it was probably the first time I'd heard that from her.

✿✿

I got up in the morning on my bed in the cottage; the other two beds had Fred and Ann sleeping on them. The bed next to me, where Christa had slept last night, was empty, with its sheet neatly done and blanket folded.

With sleepy eyes, I noticed a folded note lying in the middle of it, with 'for Ali' written over it.

I opened the paper and read.

"Most loves are like that... Your heart starts to feel like an overcrowded lifeboat. You throw your pride out to keep it afloat, and your self-respect and independence. After a while, you start throwing people out - your friends, everyone you used to know. And it's still not enough. The lifeboat is still sinking, and you

know it's going to take you down with it. I've seen that happen to a lot of people here. And that's why I'm sick of love." – Shantaram

I looked at the note for a minute, confused and trying to decipher what it meant. Fred got up rubbing his eyes and looked at me holding the paper.

"Where's Christa?" I asked him.

"Christa? She left man. She will be leaving India. Didn't she tell you?"

I looked at him with my mind going in trance. "What are you saying?" I murmured.

"She left for Italy man. Her embassy work got cleared last week. Don't you know?"

I looked at him blankly and felt numbness creeping into my body with every passing second.

"What happened man? You okay?" he asked keeping his hand on my back.

"Nothing" I said and noticed my voice choke.

"Whoa! You look disturbed buddy! Everything okay?" he asked sitting down next to me.

I remained silent and shut my eyes. Clenching my head tightly, I tried to shrug off the numbness that had taken over my mind.

"Hey Ali! You alright? What happened? Did Christa leave without telling you? Listen, snort up stuff man. No big deal, you'll have the best high ever..." Fred kept speaking as his voice drowned out and a mad cacophony of Christa's voice started ringing in my head.

I suddenly opened my eyes and got up wiping the sweat beads from my forehead.

I collected all my clothes and started stuffing them into my bag.

"Hey Ali! Where are you going?" Fred came to me and asked.

I remained silent and kept stuffing my bag hysterically collecting all my stuff strewn across the room.

"Where are you going man?" He came and tried to block my way as I strode towards the door.

"Get out of my way!" I said pushing him aside and left the cottage slamming the door behind me.

I roamed at the beach, and walked till the spot where Christa and I had come the night before. I still couldn't bring myself to believe what I had heard from Fred. I looked for her everywhere. I dialled her number but it wasn't reachable.

Later, I went and idly sat on the beach, wondering where she would be right now. I realised trying to contact her wouldn't help, because she had gone away on her will.

Everything started making sense to me. All the restraint and uneasiness in Christa's eyes all the while and the irrationality in the way this trip had happened. Fred wasn't the reason. The reason was this.

I left for Bangalore in the car. Speeding blindly on the dusty highway and smoking continuously, I tried to come to terms with reality and noticed tears in my eyes.

I looked into the rear view mirror and thought to myself that maybe I was made to be hurt in love, and had to live with it repeatedly.

Christa had left me on the brink of a little happiness that I had hoped for after a long time now. It was as if a drowning man was rescued and then pushed back into the water after getting a little breath.

I reached Bangalore and finally my apartment. It was early morning and Sandy was asleep. The walls of the house haunted me. I searched for hash in Holika's closet and found some. I smoked all of it and tried to rest my mind into sleep. Christa's face kept appearing before me and her voices echoed in my head uncontrollably. I wished I could pass out by snorting cocaine. Possibility of death by overdose didn't seem terrifying anymore.

✿✿

I started spending my days at The Jewels galleria or in front of the Central Prison, hoping to see Christa sometime, somewhere.

I spent hours standing besides the Jewels showroom, and even asked the pie vendor about Christa.

Policemen at the Central Prison could never recall whom I enquired about.

I went to the Italian embassy and wasn't let in.

Where ever I went, no one knew what I came asking for.

I went to Christa's township, almost everyone recognised me by the face, but no one knew where Christa was.

The door of her house was locked, I peeped through the keyhole to find the hall cleaned up.

Her landlord came out and told me that she paid the entire pending rent a week before vacating.

After a few days, when all my efforts to track down Christa went futile, I went back to drugs.

I started locking myself up in my room, when Sandy was out, and smoked more and more hash.

The time of never keeping sober came back to my life like déjà vu.

More work followed. I again started taking work from the validator, in addition to my own work, which made me stay in office till late hours.

Balu and Raja again became the only people I talked to at office and who gave me packets every couple of days.

Here I was, playing Jimi Hendrix's 'Castles Made of Sand' and smoking hash all through the weekends, all over again.

I barely talked to Sandy and started having brash arguments with him. He yelled at me finding out that I had been smoking up and wasting myself for days together. At times he used to sit me down and talk to me, but when nothing worked out he just shouted and yelled at me. In fit of rage he sometimes threw the joint from my hand out of the balcony. Too high and dark in my mind, I barely ever reacted to anything. Sometimes, I just looked at him, smiled and hugged him.

Sometimes while walking across the room, I glanced at the mirror. It was the same gauntly and morbid person whom I had escaped from a few months ago. Right now, I found him overpowering me beyond my control. I wanted more hash. I wanted Christa.

9

TO WHERE?

I received a call from Sandy one evening while I was lying on my bed - drunk, doped and passed out.

"Open the door" he said on the phone and it sounded like some faint sound from miles away.

"What?" I wobbled.

"Open the door you ass! I've been ringing the bell!" he shouted.

I got up, struggling to walk straight.

I reached the door balancing myself all along the way and opened it. Without looking at the person standing at the door, I turned back to my room as soon as I turned the latch open.

"Ali!" a voice called out from behind and hit like a hammer in my head.

I was high, very high, but I could recognize this voice.

There was a sudden revolt of thoughts in my head as I stood there trying to get sane and respond to it.

I turned around to look at the person. My body shivered from within the very moment I recognized the person through my fuzzy vision. The face repeatedly blurred and cleared itself in front of me.

It was Divya.

I fell to the ground; hitting my head on the floor and everything blacked out.

I woke up in my bed; there was no one around in the room. My head ached from within and that added to the pain of the hit I had taken. I stood up and went to the mirror to check the bruise. I looked hideous. My body frame seemed rickety; my eyes were poppy and there was an awkwardly swelled up bump on my forehead.

I walked out of the room and saw Sandy and Hoilka sitting in the hall. I tried not look into Sandy's disdainful eyes and walked to the on the other side of the room, pretending to reach out for the TV remote.

I looked up and suddenly it struck me that Divya was sitting on the other couch. I looked at her and confirmed to myself that it wasn't a nightmare.

I looked into her eyes with a blank, thoughtless mind. She looked down and probably tried to get a reaction from me but I just kept looking. After few seconds, she came towards me and hugged me tight.

"What happened?" I asked plainly, trying to get her off me.

"I'm sorry Ali. I'm sorry." She said and burst out crying.

I calmly got her off me and walked back to my room.

I heard Sandy and Holika trying to pacify her into stop crying but she didn't stop.

She cried to the extent of almost losing her breath. Sandy got her in my room as I sat on my bed; it pained me to hear her cry so badly. I looked at her bloodshot eyes and tears streaming down her face. She was still the same, her face and those big black eyes bought back all the memories we had shared in a moment.

She had just one thing to say, "I'm sorry"

I knew that if I would move forward and hug her, she would stop crying and the chaos in the house would be over.

But I realised I didn't want to do it, even for the sake of it, 'cause that's how bad love happens, you go for it in an urge, and then go into it more making all kinds of promises, and then you realise you never really wanted to do it.

Sandy somehow pacified her to come with him, and dropped her to her house.

He came back and asked me to come to the balcony.

"What's wrong with you Ali? Did you see the way she was crying?" he asked, almost shouting at me.

"So what do I do about it?" I asked him plainly, looking out from the balcony.

"What the fuck have you got attitude about you asshole!" he said pulling me to turn towards him.

"I don't know Sandy. I can't forget Christa."

"Christa? Wow! You gotta be kidding me man. She went where she had to. What else did you expect? She went to her country, that's where she belong Ali. What has gotten into you? That was a fling. Just a fling! This is Divya!"

"I don't know. I'm happy the way I am. All by myself."

"Happy all by yourself? Look at you! You're back to square one Ali. You look fucked up again. You smoke up all the time in your room and you never really talk sane. You're miserable right now. And you're more miserable without Divya. Life rarely gives us second chance Ali. God has given you a chance to reform yourself again..."

He kept talking and suddenly stopped seeing me uninterested and aloof to all that he was saying.

"Listen to me for God's sake Ali. She's waiting for you. Forgive her and get back with her. That's how it should be!" he said and left.

Later, Sandy did best to make me listen and spoke a lot that night. Clouded by doubtfulness about where my life was heading, if not into a downward slope to nowhere, I convinced myself to get back with Divya.

Sandy drove her to our apartment next day in the evening when I came back from work.

I was sitting in my room when he opened the door and said, "Ali, she's here". He moved away and Divya entered.

Her eyes were puffy and red, and she was again on the verge of breaking down.

"Please don't cry." I said.

She didn't reply and came and sat at the corner of my bed.

"It all went wrong. So terribly wrong. I don't even know what to do except just cry and say sorry" she said after a moment.

"Divya, I don't really know everything can be way it was before. It's been long, and a lot has happened ever since"

"I know, Sandy told me" she said.

"What did he tell you?" I asked.

"Your miserable condition after we separated, why did you do this to yourself Ali?"

"Let me rephrase it, why did you do it to me Divya?" I said looking at her straight in the eyes.

"I got carried away, I'm sorry Ali" she started crying again. "I was alone there, in the US, and things just happened one over another, I didn't get time to even stop over and think" she said through her sobs.

"And you ended it all by just one mail?"

"I was so stupid. I want our old times back Ali, what do I do now? How do I apologise?" she said and came forward and hugged me.

I hugged her back and she frantically cried lying over me.

We kissed and tried to bring back our old desires in. She repeatedly forced herself over me and encouraged me to love her back again like the way I used to.

I tried but everything was reminding me of Christa, I tried to remember Sandy's words that she went where she had to and it was just a fling, but a part of me didn't relent to any of it.

She came to my ear and whispered though her soft sobbing, 'I love you'.

It sent a sudden disturbance thru my mind, but I hugged her back. After a while, she went to sleep.

I got up in the morning and dressed up for office.

I looked at Divya's sleeping face and tried to brush off the usual restlessness in my mind and the troubled air in my room, but nothing seemed different.

I went to the office with hundreds of thoughts ringing in my head, and asked myself what love really is, could I call falling for an Italian girl in a few days of our meeting love, or was it getting back what I once called true love.

Christa's last words on the beach still ringed in my head, 'I love you', and they disturbed me every single time.

I knew she wouldn't have faked it. And I hoped I wasn't faking it with Divya.

✿✿

Days went by and Divya came back in my life like before. We went out to the movies, spend time together whenever we could, and from a distance, people said I was getting back to normal.

But when I looked into the mirror and took a moment to think about myself, I could feel I was still the same miserable me.

I went to The Jewels with Divya and spend time with her the same way I used to with Christa, and all that while, I realised I was actually searching for Christa in her, and everywhere.

At times when Divya found me too quiet, she asked me if I was okay, I used to smile and hug her, and still try harder to be with her and see my life ahead with her.

But as days went by, I realised my intimacy with Divya didn't mean anything to me.

How much ever I tried, I couldn't get back to be normal with her. Whenever we got intimate and close, more than anything, it was the hundreds of questions that I wanted to ask her. To which I knew she didn't have any answers to.

✿✿

After a few days, when I was in office, I went to Michael's cabin to submit my work and found him yelling at someone on the phone, "In such a short notice? You should've told me before! How do I convince anyone here now? Impossible man, impossible. I'll send out a mail to everyone but don't expect anything" He shouted and disconnected.

"What happened?" I asked.

"Nothing, Delhi office needs one person on urgent basis, my team there is falling short on one person and they've an audit visit in three days. This is crazy man. You know anyone who can relocate to Delhi on such short notice?" he asked.

"Yes" I said.

"Really? Who?!" he asked.

"Me" I said.

"You? Are you out of your mind?"

"I don't know, but I don't mind going" I said.

He looked at me in a confused expression and asked, "But why do you want to go all of a sudden?"

"Just like that" I said and remained quiet.

After a while he sighed and asked, "If you really are serious, let me know when you can move."

"Tomorrow." I said and left.

Michael asked me a lot later, that why I wanted to shift. I didn't tell him about the turmoil in my life, but told him that I had my parents in Delhi, and they were eager to see me come home permanently.

I didn't know what I was doing, and didn't ask anyone either. I just pounced at an opportunity to run away from the life that I had built for myself.

I didn't know what lied ahead of me, and didn't care about it either. I just got a chance to give myself a chance, and I took it.

Packing guys came to my house the next day and packed all of my stuff in a few hours.

Sandy silently stood in one corner and expressionlessly looked at everything happening. He surprisingly never questioned my sudden decision to move to Delhi. I think he had given up on me by now.

"Give this to Divya" I said and gave him the note that Christa had given me. I hadn't told Divya anything, and felt that the quote in the letter would suffice what I really wanted to convey to her, that I was 'sick of love'.

I hugged Sandy hard, and for a moment felt like never letting him go.

I wanted to live all of my memories with him again. From the first day at college, when we had reluctantly told each other our names, to our marijuana sessions, to our night rides on the old RX 100, and to finally this day. Everything little thing flashed fervently in my mind and tears surfaced my eyes.

I finally bid him and Holika bye as Balu honked in the cab.

The cab rolled.

And thus, teary eyed and broken hearted, I looked back the apartment building for the last time and said one of the hardest ever goodbyes of my life.

10

SICK OF LOVE

Delhi greeted me with loud laughter and chatter all around me at the airport. I walked to the exit, pulling my trolley and making my way through people shouting into their phones and almost announcing to the whole crowd around that they've landed in Delhi.

The cab and taxi men stood stuck to the barricades along the exit walkway, some of them leaning over to grab a hold of my hand, shouting and asking me where I wanted to go, I wanted to tell them that I'd travelled across the country on pure whim, and was still looking for an answer to that question.

I took a turn at the walkway where the barricades ended. A middle-aged, pot bellied man came and stood in front of me.

He held his head up a little, and asked "Taxi?", speaking

mumbly by making a bowl out of his mouth which was heavily loaded with red chewed tobacco.

I nodded and he swiftly took the luggage trolley from my hand.

"Come with me, new to *Dilli*?" he asked me again struggling to speak clearly.

I didn't answer; busy looking around and already sweltering under the hot sun.

He led me to his old weary cab, and pulled open the creaking door for me.

The speakers blasted with *Punjabi* music, and the cab rolled.

I looked out of the window and lit a cigarette. The roads bought back memories of my childhood spent in Delhi.

The cab went past children's park near India Gate and I pictured my dad pushing me on the swing in the park years ago and the happiness that I got through that.

The lollipops had now transformed into cigarettes, and the only happiness I now knew came in form of packets sold for hundred bucks in the shady streets near Bangalore Railway Station.

The *Punjabi* singer roared in the background. He seemed to be giving an advice in his song. The lyrics have him crazily begging the listener to not let yourself fall into the trap of love, and to not hear what your heart says, because it somehow shall and will make you digress into the dark streets of love. He gives a clear choice, between love and happiness, asserting the fact that you can't have both indefinitely.

"*Oye pencho!*" a loud shriek from outside the car cut through my thoughts. I looked at the driver, he had rolled down the window and had spat a red streak from his mouth dangerously close to a motorist, who gave him the word in return.

The driver turned towards me, "Welcome to *Dilli* sir, everyone on the road is a *pencho* here" he said with a wide grin. Before I could respond, he turned back to the road and shouted the slang at another motorist, for coming in way of our waywardly going cab.

The noisy ride continued past many memories of Delhi, occasionally disturbing me with slang and squeaking brakes.

"Here you are, Sir" the driver said turning towards me as I noticed that the car had almost reached my house.

They say in the end, everybody goes back to their own lives. I looked at the building of my house and wondered how I'd gone through a complete circle, stuffing all my stuff in an iron trunk and leaving this very same alley eight years ago. Today I'd come back, amongst other things, I'd the very same iron trunk coming back with me, I hoped it was as easy as that to get myself back in the life that I'd left, and was now expected to come back to.

"Rafiq" the driver's voice again cut through my thoughts as the car stood still in front of my house.

"What?" I asked him as his hand stretched out towards me with his mouth again filled with newer red liquid.

"Rafiq, the name is Rafiq" he said, again struggling to speak, but never hesitating.

"Ali" I said and shook his hand firmly with a smile.

He returned a wider one, and the one which dangerously but skilfully managed the contents inside his mouth.

I realised I'd taken an instant liking to him, he cared to smile his heart out at me, and cared to talk to me throughout the journey despite my limited replies and the effort he needed to speak clearly.

"New to *Dilli*?" he asked the same question that he'd asked in start of the journey.

"Yes and no" I answered.

"Take my card. I can be helpful in both the cases, Sir" he said and gave me his visiting card.

Minutes later, I stood at the porch in front of my house. I could have told mom and dad that I'd arrived and they'd have rushed out of the door to see me, but I wanted to breathe easy and take a moment out to myself.

I realised that this was my safe zone, this was where I could easily come back to, these are the people who accepted me for my bad more than my good, infact they didn't care to know any of that, they were just there, by default, and they were there to make this world an easier place for you.

More so because they won't leave you, they won't leave philosophical notes on the table for you in the morning and be gone that way.

They give you a safe zone which makes you hate yourself for being into, and hate yourself more for not help but accept the fact that you came back to it only when you needed it.

My days at home started with a monotonous routine of eating and sleeping. My mother wanted to shower me with love and care whenever she would get a chance, she always had something to cook for me, and something to show me on the TV and talk hours at length about relatives that I had forgotten existed. I sat through it all, mostly napping on her lap and occasionally trying to register some of it, but my mind always wandered, it wandered into a blurred vision of the empty hall, into the long stretched road and a creaking RX 100, pictures of central prison and a scent that filled the car that day, a cat climbing over my shoulder, an Italian woman shouting over the phone, and the waves from the beach hitting my naked body.

After three days of being at home, I went to the Delhi office. Michael messaged me in the morning wishing me a good start.

Unlike a cab, this time the transport was a bus, which had most of the people inside sleeping when I entered.

The bus moved with a jerk. I reclined the seat and shut my eyes. And thus started my journey into Delhi, sleepy and bumpy, with me willing to pick up the broken pieces and build back the castle, this time hopefully not made of sand.

My boss was an imposingly gregarious man, with a tall, almost hounding demeanour. The huge but neatly done turban on his head added to his height and most of his face hid behind his thick beard. His loud laughter seemed like an echo coming out of somewhere deep within his persona, and he rarely did away with it.

"This is Ali, new to our team guys" he announced to the people sitting on their desks across an area in the office, most of them seemingly uninterested in any of what was happening around.

Soon I found a corner desk and was loaded with work, I had to do it all with a deadline of the audit, and with no one to talk to.

I started working, mostly concentrating on work and keeping to myself, and soon started syncing into project deadlines and an impending external audit.

"Our new boy shouldn't work so hard. Go home for today Ali, we will handle everything" my boss Hardeep Singh, or Harry as he was liked to be called, came and patted on my back.

It was nine into the night, but as usual I didn't had anything to do at home, or more so anything to do with my life. So sitting in the brightly lit office and crunching numbers through computer programs had become the most meaningful thing I could do with my life.

"Just this last one Harry, then I leave"

I worked for an hour more and left office with few people still working. The popular discotheque near the office building had the crowd just gathered for the night to begin.

As usual an assortment of contoured and labelled cars with blaring music stretched across the length of the road, there were guys and girls hooting and laughing with no worry of the world. Walking past them, in office attire and with a laptop bag slung across my shoulder, I felt a phase of my life, whose reminiscences were playing right next to me, had come to an end. It's always hard to accept that life has phases and even if we would want to stay over a little more in any one of them, nobody cares and soon we find ourselves thrown out once it's timeout.

I reached home with a usual throbbing headache, ate my food and went to bed. Like every other night, tired and half asleep, I felt the breeze on the beach that night, felt the darkness in the car in the parking lot, and felt the heavy rain drenching me as I leaned against the wall.

I wondered where Christa would be right now, and what would she be doing, would she be in a party with a guy next to her, or in bed on a lonely night with similar thoughts as mine going through her head.

I drifted off to the usual black, numb sleep.

Days in office were getting increasingly toiling as the audit date approached. When others cribbed about and avoided long work hours, I strangely found myself willingly sitting through long work hours. Work became a tool to wade off the loneliness in the vastness of the new city and the training that my mind needed to not to think about the life I had left behind.

Sometimes, I randomly googled Christa's name and everything that I had collected about her in the few days of our togetherness. I searched Italian directories, translating them into English through online softwares. They listed loads of Christas, and looking at each name with a phone number next to it, I wondered if dialling one of the numbers would make me hear her voice. Sometimes I randomly dialled a few numbers and knew it wasn't her at the first word from the other side.

It was torturous; to unreasonably expect her voice every time there was a ring, and then get to hear some random stranger from the other side of the world. Sometimes I used to irritatingly thump down the phone, amidst stares and murmurs from the colleagues around.

Everyone knew that I'm messed up and tangled into myself, but nobody ever asked me anything.

Divya mailed me at times. I replied to her mails for the sake of informing her about my whereabouts, but could never go beyond that. She always had questions that I had no answers to. She asked me why I did what I did and where I was headed in life. They were the same questions that I had been asking myself and they echoed in my mind almost everyday. I understood her pain like my own, she had been left deserted and had to live with it. I also understood that being with her led me to betterment and was like a mortar filling into the hollowness of my life. But it never doused the restlessness and turmoil in my head. I lived with the risk of living with that turmoil forever, but I still chose it and lived on.

I looked to vent out that turmoil by keeping myself busy through work and late night stays in office. I sometimes immersed myself in my workstation for hours together, and deliberately exhausted my mind to the extent of not being able to think of anything after I left for home. Through all of that, I was merely trying to wade off the never ending thoughts of Christa playing in my mind, day in and day out, and I failed at it every single day, miserably and helplessly.

I still sometimes went to Paharganj on weekends. Aimlessly roaming on the crowded and chaotic streets, I strolled past all the budget hotels and eateries where foreigners hung around. Hounded by the usual loneliness that I had now learnt to live with, I scanned each and every face around, knowing that it will be futile as always but still protecting the silent desperation I had developed in a corner of my mind, which was an incessant hope of spotting Christa chatting away in one of the groups around, with her same echoing laughter that still sometimes woke me up in the middle of the night.

Though I had accepted the fact that she was thousands of miles away from where I was, perhaps even having erased the slightest memory of me from her mind, but I still came to these streets to unwillingly flutter into that curbed desperation. Maybe it was the thought of being at the same place where she once was, and living the same life that she had once lived, even though for just a few hours.

I let myself go miserable with each visit to those streets, and willingly continued to nurture the silent desperation that I knew will not take me anywhere.

At work, as I worked harder and harder, sometimes sitting up till the wee hours, Harry picked me up for the presentation to be given to auditors. After managing to deliver a fair presentation and setting everything on smooth course, I was applauded at the office party and was eventually promoted.

At the office party, amidst applause and pats on my back, I got to know a few more people and befriended some of them.

Regular outings with office friends started eating into the long ridden loneliness and bitterness that had infested my life. I started going to bars and pubs with boisterous group of friends from office. Watching football on huge LCDs, raising my beer mug high up in the air and joining the loud laughter coming up at every single thing anyone popped from their mouth became my regular weekend schedule.

It wasn't the best of time I used to have; in fact it was an outright façade, a mere therapy that I was pushing in into my mind, incessantly convincing myself that it was working. I forcibly started counting these people as my friends, ignoring my mind telling me that I didn't fit in this life. I read self-help books lent out to me and fooled a part of myself that I liked them for the philosophy of being happy that the author imposed upon readers.

I rarely knew the occasion but I never rejected an invite for any party in town where I was invited due to series of common friends. I went to these parties and shared fake smiles and met more people whom I added to the kitty that I now called friends.

I started sleeping over at places of random people who were distant common friends, and sometimes woke up in the afternoon all alone in a messed up house.

All along this, I was chasing more and more chaos in the name of fun and treated it as a therapy to all the silent and lonely time I had spent. At times, chatting with attractive women over a glass of wine at a party, and sometimes even looking to make a way with them into the night, I could feel a part of me telling me that this was it, I had moved over Christa and to hell with the thousands of thoughts that had gnawed me from inside day in and day out. But then at the very same moment another part of me dominated everything and rekindled Christa's face right in front of my eyes. All that I incessantly tried to get over for days together went futile in a single moment of realisation.

I kept ignoring that voice, kept ignoring the conflicting thoughts and the monstrous memory vault in my head, and kept living with the hope of finding order of life in all the chaos I was submerging myself in.

As days after days ended, and evenings after evenings, after-office parties piled up one after another. I lost myself more and more in the bedlam, and gave into the deliberately constructed idea in my mind that I had now incredibly moved on from all that I had ever suffered. I started protecting that idea more than anything, for I understood how delicate it was and all I needed was one bad memory to shatter it right away.

Months went by and the dark cloud around me got stronger, eventually phasing the old me out of my sight.

In the raves, the girls threw themselves at me, sometimes for as little as a couple of drinks, and as a result I entered and exited multiple flings, some of them lasting not longer than a night. Through them, I tried to convince myself that my days with Christa were one of such experiences, but the meaningless short flings and casual sex filled more bitterness into my life for which I soon started detesting my own self.

It was getting difficult to have a foresight through the thick haze of faceless crowd and jamboree I had chosen for myself.

The preconceived notions of using this life as an escape route and a therapy stopped making sense to me anymore.

I looked in the mirror and recoiled in disgust at my own self for the snake-pit into which I was spiralling myself down. But escaping from this new vicious circle left just one option to me, to drown back into the old loneliness and depression that I had been running away from and had been unsuccessful from the word go.

More days went by and in the same unsuccessful quest of forgetting the past; I kept foraging into darker streets of despair and chaos which now seemed like a big Lonesome Town to me. As Ricky Nelson had sung back in the 60s,

"There's a place where lovers go,
To cry their troubles away.
And they call it Lonesome Town,
Where the broken hearts stay.

In this town of broken dreams,
The streets are filled with regret.
Maybe down in Lonesome Town,
I can learn to forget."

11

LEARNING TO FORGET
(One year later)

I woke up to the loud wakeup call from Venkat, one of my colleagues whose place I had woken up at.

"What time is it?" I asked rubbing my eyes.

"It's nine already. We need to rush to office Ali. Client meeting today" he said and disappeared into the washroom.

I looked at the clock and realised I was sufficiently late for office. Within next few minutes, I shaved, showered and dressed up in neat, ironed formals, fishing a pair out of the few I had kept at his place for mornings like these.

After a heavy breakfast, I popped a headache pill to wade off the hangover from last night and set out for office.

More than an year had passed since I had moved to Delhi. In the course of past one year, I had comfortably learnt to live in the Lonesome Town that I had constructed around myself. Forgetting Christa was easy now, as I vaguely remembered what my own self was an year back in time.

Behind the image of a dull, snobbish corporate slave, complete with a slight beer paunch and a sole aim of making money in the day and whiling it away into the night, I had hidden away the Ali that existed an year ago.

I had settled into a silent agreement with the reflection in my mirror to not interfere in my life. I met that reflection every morning, recognised it to a slight extent, and tried not to let our eyes meet for long. I knew I had to get back to him, or he soon will overpower this pretentious me, but I continued not giving him many chances, and making him feel miserable with every ignorance I meted out to him.

In a corner of my mind, I knew I was a faker, and it was really me who was miserable, wretched and weak and was probably beyond any repair now. But till all of it kept me away from the thoughts I had gotten over after the yearlong effort, I was ready to keep living in this continuous flutter and turmoil which now was my life.

Christa had become a faint memory by now. Something which seemed like a grained reminisce going back ages in time. Behind the pulse of dark rave parties, forgotten faces of the women I woke up with, and bitter hangovers morning after morning, Christa's bright, lively face still sometimes shimmered at a distance in my mind. There was a calm, tranquil smile on that face, in a way which almost mocked at me. And the gaze, through all the commotion, looked at me directly in the eye. I could never wade it off, through the days and nights, which hollowed me from within and parched my soul, I could still see the gaze looking at me in the eye.

After getting promoted at office, I did not have much work to do, and always assigned a part of my work to my juniors. Some of them even perceived me as a sadist, who derived his sense of superiority by bossing around with them. I barely got to office on time, and when there were big parties and meetups in the evenings, I used to exit early by loading them with all my work. I didn't share any connect with them and it didn't affect me either. I knew I had now transformed into a bad performer and made other people around me too hate their work, these realizations disturbed me deep down under, but I just carried on, too far ahead and too tangled to stop over and pay heed to these things which were just a small part of the ever burgeoning problems I had with my own conscience.

But as they say, 'every saint has a past and every sinner has a future', I too had a future waiting out there for me. One which was too hazed out to be deciphered through my ignorance and worn out conscience. One day, it all came down on me. The future that I thought I had mixed up in my cocktail and downed my throat a long time back, came my way and tore away the blindfold off my eyes. It hit me with a hammering force, violently jerking me out of my long, forgotten sleep.

One day, the path I was spiralling down hit a dead end, clearing out all the haze and chaos in a single moment, and changed my life forever.

"Ali! Dude! Wake up!" I woke up at Venkat's house yet again. It was a Saturday and India had won the cricket world cup the night before.

I woke up with a throbbing headache and adjusted my eyes to the piercing sunrays entering the room.

"Last night was crazy man! Everyone was so damn wasted after India won" Venkat said getting me a bottle of water.

"Yeah" I responded and quenched my thirst. I couldn't recall how I got to Venkat's house after the party at a popular discotheque the night before. It was usual and I didn't bother recalling or asking Venkat.

Lazing on the bed, I picked up the TV remote lying close to me and switched on the TV. With my eyes still squinted and adjusting to the light, I lay flat on my bed and randomly flicked channels on the TV.

I casually stopped at a channel and kept down the remote to light a cigarette. With no specific thought crossing my mind, I smoked and looked at the TV screen still lying flat on the bed.

The program playing on the screen had a couple of wild cats chasing down on a prey. I yawned and continued smoking, bounded by the general morning hangover lethargy that was a regular for me.

As I watched the screen thoughtlessly for a few more minutes, too lazy to reach out for the remote and flick over to another channel, there was an advertisement.

What I saw next froze me.

"In the next episode of Jailed Abroad, see how an Italian woman on an extended work-vacation in India is caught drug smuggling and ends up in the biggest prison in South Asia"

The words from the TV advert crept over me as I watched the screen in horror. They show the mug shot of the woman and run audio clips from her documentary interview in the backdrop.

The cigarette in my hand dropped. My throat went dry. The woman is Christa.

I looked around in shock and sprang up from the bed to make sure I wasn't in a dream.

Too appalled to react or come to terms with what had just flashed in front of my eyes, I ran to my office bag and opened my laptop.

"Jailed Up Abroad Episode 9: See how Christa Matthews ends up in an Asian jail after being caught smuggling drugs in India." the webpage of the program on the channel website flashed, with the same forty-five second video that I had seen on TV.

I paused the video where they show the mug shot for a second amongst a collage of images. I looked hard into the hazy low resolution video. Shiver ran down my body as I confirmed it was Christa. In the grainy image, she held a placard scribbled with her name and some unreadable text.

I was in a zone. My heart was pounding and sweat beads developed on my forehead. I again stared hard into the hazy image in the paused video and again conformed to myself that it was Christa. She looked blankly into the camera with a morbid, expressionless face.

Still under the shock, I took my eyes off the screen and clenched my head hard. A million thoughts flooded my mind. I shut my eyes and tried to make sense of the commotion in my head. The memories from past one year flashed through my mind and cleared the haze I had built around myself.

I recalled Christa's face from the last I time I had seen her, and recalled the old me that was miserable without her. The words from the TV, 'Christa Matthews ends up in an Asian jail after being caught smuggling drugs in India' resounded in my head and the reality of it came crashing down on me all at once.

I picked up the bottle and poured the water over my head.

Of all the shock, confusion and disorderly thoughts, there

was only one thing I could think straight - Wherever Christa was, I had to find her.

❀❀

I searched the internet endlessly for hours, and expected some information apart from the channel website which pertained to Christa. Nothing came up.

Jailed Up Abroad was a soon to be started British documentary drama series, the channel website stated. Apart from the teaser video whose featuring date was titled 'Coming Soon', there was nothing on the website.

I kept searching in futility, coupling Christa Matthews with random words like jail, crime, drugs and smuggling.

There was nothing.

When it was late into the night and I was still at Venkat's place, not having moved away from the laptop since morning, I was tired and had a throbbing headache. The shock and disbelief had still not faded away from my mind.

I thought of approaching the Italian Embassy for Christa's whereabouts, and in corner of my mind was still hoping that the program was some sort of sensationalism. Maybe Christa would have goofed up something while in Italy and spent a night in jail. But then it struck me that the video had the words 'biggest prison in South Asia'.

I googled the words. The search results sent tremors down my body. The jail was Tihar. 'Tihar Prisons: Largest Prison Complex in South Asia', the search results flashed.

I looked at the screen going numb in my mind.

Tihar Jail was right in the heart of Delhi. If I was to believe the video, Christa was locked up in Tihar Jail, which was few kilometres away from where I currently was.

I shut the laptop lid down and let out a heavy sigh. It was difficult to accept all the facts suddenly hurled at me. The thought of Christa spending her days in a squalid prison cell few kilometres away from me all this while set off an uncontrollable panic in my head.

I went to the washroom and repeatedly splashed water on my face. Ignoring the tears surfacing my eyes, I looked at my face in the dingy washroom mirror. It reflected helplessness and a strange guilt that made me loath my own reflection. A boisterous group of people entered the house, I could hear their voices, some of them asked Venkat about me while some asked where the booze was. One of them called out my name, asking me to come to the hall and join them. Probably it was another party at Venkat's place. Soon everyone would be drunk and loud hoots of laughter would echo around. As a norm I would pass out in the hall itself or would manage to walk back to the room. This was my life. And probably the most significant part of it.

Someone called out my name again, asking me to join them soon and that the booze would be over. Soon all the voices drowned out to loud music.

Tired and dejected, and almost on the verge of breaking down, I came back to the room and curled up into the bed.

Amid the blaring music and voices, I tried to let some peace seep into my head. I thought of going out to the hall and getting drunk and doped, but nothing seemed like an option to quell the havoc that thoughts of Christa had created in my mind.

I had a million questions hounding me. I closed my eyes and felt like endlessly falling into a dark abyss filled with those questions.

Someone played *'Hello darkness, my old friend. I've come to talk with you again'* in the hall.

Amid the incessant flashes of Christa's face and depressing drone of the song, I tried to drift my mind into slumber.

12

HELLO DARKNESS

"What?! Tihar Jail?!" Venkat retorted when I told him where I wanted him to accompany me.

"Don't yell! I will tell you everything." I whispered calming him down as people turned around from their seats to look at both of us.

It had been three days since I had seen Christa in the TV advert. I had been searching more and more of web, and still stumbling upon nothing except the page on the channel website. I had almost memorised the words from the short video by now, running it several times a day and just seeing through each second of it every single time.

Common sense told me that it might take any number of days for the channel to air the full documentary on their website or TV, as it still showed a Coming Soon tag and the page was created not more than a week back.

It was getting difficult for me to get the cacophony of voices out of my mind. At the day time, whether in office or at home, my mind could not drift away from the mug shot of Christa holding the placard for a single moment. At night, I slept with those thoughts pulling me down into darkness and depression.

I had stopped responding to calls and texts. And in the corner of my mind, I was still grappling to come out of the shock.

"But why?" Venkat replied. This time not yelling, but attracting glances nevertheless.

"Don't get worked up! It's nothing. Let's go out for a walk. I will tell you everything." I said and we both quietly walked out.

"See, today evening, can you come with me to that place?" I asked Venkat when we had walked out of the office.

"Which place?" he asked.

"Same place that I just told you in office"

"Tihar Jail?"

"Yes"

"You mean The Tihar Jail? The prison?"

"What else can it mean?"

"You mean today evening you will go inside Tihar Jail and I will come with you?"

"Exactly"

"Okay" he replied and kept looking at me expressionlessly.

"And do you mind telling me the reason now?" he asked after a moment.

"There is a big reason. And there's nothing to worry. You just have to accompany me" I replied as we had reached the smoking corner.

I tried to offer Venkat a cigarette hoping to calm him down.

"Okay. You want me to visit Tihar Jail with you saying it's nothing. And you wouldn't tell me the reason too. This sounds so rational." he said lighting a cigarette.

"Yes. So you agree? Nice"

"What?! Fuck you! I am not going to any Tihar Jail with you buddy. You better tell me the reason clearly and then let me tell you what I agree to and what I don't!"

"Okay. Calm down. And listen, an old friend of mine is locked up there. I want to meet her as a visitor. That's all."

He looked at me blankly and did not reply.

"What? Say something! We'll just go as visitors. What's wrong with that? Wouldn't visitors go there all the time?" I asked waving at him.

"Dude. Are you serious?" he replied after a moment.

"Yes I am. Why are you so psyched out? Trust me it's no big deal"

"No big deal? Might not be a big deal for you. I have never visited Tihar Jail man. In fact any goddamn jail. So it sure is a very big deal for me."

"Neither have I" I said.

"Neither have you what?" he asked.

"Visited a jail. Any goddamn jail." I replied.

"What?!"

"Yes"

"Wait. You mean you have never been there?'

"No"

"What the fuck does that mean?! How can you just go there if..."

"Listen" I said cutting him short, "We'd go there, meet someone and try to figure out how to meet an inmate. Okay?"

"No way in hell! Fuck you!"

✿✿

Venkat and I set out for Tihar at around six in the evening. While Venkat still whined sitting next to me in the car, my heart ponded in my chest as I drove the car and we approached closer to area where the jail was.

The area is called Hari Nagar. I drove into the lane with a direction board directing towards Hari Nagar. The area looked like any other residential area in Delhi. It was quiet and calm with pedestrians walking around and few shops intermingled with row houses.

I drove further and there it was. A big direction board inscribed with 'Tihar Central Prison' and an arrow mark towards left.

I took the left turn and stooped down to look at the surroundings and the road ahead. It was cold and Delhi was foggy at nights. The area was deserted, dark and unnervingly quiet. With apprehension and chill going down my spine, I drove further.

"Whoa! Are we going in? Do you know where are we heading?" Venkat snapped up.

"I don't know. Looks like the way to the jail" I replied looking around the area.

"What?! Way to the jail? Fuck you man. You don't know anything! Pull over. Pull over now!" Venkat shouted and leaned over towards the steering to reach the key.

"I don't want to get locked up! Look at this area! We can get mugged you ass!" he continued shouting as I tried to calm him down and slowly drove further into the road.

"Wow! Look we're good" I said as I saw some policeman manning a police check post and a huge road barrier under dim yellow street lamps lining the road.

"Shit! Police! Ali! Get serious man! We shouldn't be doing this!" Venkat retorted.

"Nothing will happen. Relax! We aren't criminals." I said as our car slowly approached the barrier. The policemen were all looking at us as we got closer to them. Some of them stood up and came near the barricade.

As we approached closer, and Venkat went from hysterical to numb, a policeman started signalling towards our slow moving car, waving with both his hands and asking us halt much before the barrier.

We stopped at an instant and he came trotting towards us.

My heart paced faster but I tried to keep my cool. Venkat looked expressionless.

The policeman came and leaned over the window.

For a moment of unsettling silence, we both looked at his face protruding into the car and he looked back at us.

"Open your mouth" he said suddenly.

"What?" I asked in a shaking voice.

"Open your mouth and breathe out!" he shouted at us.

I opened my mouth and breathed out at his face. He walked to the other side and Venkat did the same.

He said something on this radio-phone and signalled us to step out of the car.

"Are you both drunk?" he asked as soon as we got out.

"No. No Sir. Not at all." Venkat replied in a frightened voice.

"What is the matter?" said a sturdy voice from behind us. We turned around to find another policeman who was a seemingly superior officer staring at us. He looked annoyed and held me tightly by my arm.

"Who are you and what do you want?" he said looking at me straight in the eyes.

"Sir, I..." I said and stopped. My heartbeat raced as his clench didn't loosen and I tried hard to find reasonable words to tell him what two seemingly clueless youngsters were doing right next to a maximum security prison on a cold winter night.

"I asked you something!" He shouted in my face.

"Sir we had come here to meet a friend. We're not criminals Sir. You might be mistaken." Venkat shouted from behind.

He thankfully let go his grip off my hand and walked towards Venkat, "Meet a friend? Here?" he asked.

"Not my friend. His friend Sir." Venkat said signalling towards me, in a voice that implied that he had shit his pants.

"Whosesoevers' friend it might be! Why did you want to meet him here? This is the Central Jail area which you people are trespassing!" he shouted in our face.

"Sir but..." Venkat spoke and suddenly stopped. He looked at me, screaming with his eyes asking me to speak up.

"Sir, the friend that we want to meet is in the jail." I said.

There was silence. The officer looked at me with his eyes wide open and anger raging on his face.

Venkat was too shocked to speak up.

"Sir, my friend is lodged in the jail. In the women's jail. I had come to meet the officers so that I can meet her. He is just accompanying me." I said stammering.

"What? You people have come to meet an inmate? Like this? At this time? Here?" the officer shouted, raising his voice with his every question.

"Sir I told him he can't go just like that. Please let us go Sir we are sorry." Venkat said almost begging in his tone.

"Sorry? Sorry for trespassing high security area? You guys think it's a joke?" he shouted again.

"Frisk them. Frisk the car also" the officer directed the constable.

He hurried towards the car and started checking it thoroughly. I silently prayed there wasn't any old beer bottle or packet of weed lying in the boot. I knew Venkat was praying the same.

After flinging open all the doors and the boot, he announced that the car was clean.

I let out a sigh. Venkat looked at me, his eyes exuding a loud "Thank God!"

The constable then frisked us and signalled towards the officer that we were clean.

"Tell me the truth! Why were you here? Tell me!" the officer again shouted at us.

"Sir, I guarantee you we're good people. We came to meet his friend Sir. She is in the prison so we..."

"Shut up!" the officer cut short Venkat. His loud thud seemed to rattle through Venkat's frail body.

"Do you think you can just walk in here and meet any prisoner? Are you people out of your mind? Or you did some *charars ganja*?"

"No Sir. No drugs. We are good guys. We don't even drink." Venkat retorted.

I would have doubled up on the road if it weren't the situation.

"Okay okay. Stop the bullshit you two. Show me your driving licence" he said signalling towards me.

I handed him out. He asked the constable to write my name and licence number on his notepad.

"You, you have any ID?" the officer turned towards Venkat.

He hastily searched his walled and handed him out a card. The constable took it and jotted down the details.

"Let me search tomorrow. If I see any history on any of you, I will then teach you the hard way" the officer said and gave us both a hard look.

There was silence. Venkat looked at me while they both looked at each other.

"Now what are you waiting for? Get out of here!" the officer said.

Venkat ran into the car and signalled me to come in.

"Sir, what is the procedure for meeting an inmate of the prison?" I asked the officer hesitantly as he was waiting for me to get in the car and drive back.

"That is not my job. Go do all the enquiry yourself and come. Now get out of this place! Didn't you hear me the first time?" he said going back into his shouting mode.

I silently got in the car and drove back.

As we reached the main road, out of the dark restricted area, I saw Venkat chanting prayers for the first time. His hysterical chanting went on for a minute or so when he suddenly snapped at me, "You retard! I told you! I fuckin' told you!"

"I'm sorry." I said and remained silent for the rest of the ride, with discreet thoughts of the alley leading to the prison and Christa overcoming the leftovers of the strenuous encounter we had with the cops.

Venkat, noticing me unusually quiet, asked me if I was alright.

"Don't worry dude. This was nothing. We would find her. Fuck the cops!" he said landing his skeletal arm on my back.

"Yeah. Let's hope so" I mumbled.

I reached home late that night and retired into the bed right away.

I thought about the sight of the dark narrow road manned by policemen and wondered if Christa really was there inside the prison. It seemed unreal to me that Christa was spending her days in the prison. Chances were that her embassy would have bailed her out long back and the TV program was just some blown up news.

But I wanted to know. Anything could be sensationalism but not the mugshot which showed clearly Christa holding a placard with a height scale in the backdrop.

It disturbed me. More than her thoughts had ever disturbed me in the past one year. There were bouts when I told myself that leaving Christa be was better. Leaving her right where she was, Tihar or Itlay or anywhere, and carry on with my life. And then in a corner of my mind I would inadvertently hope that I would walk into Tihar Jail and find Christa there. Right in front of me. I would soon snap out of the thoughts and feel disgusted at myself.

I wanted to find Christa, the restlessness didn't let me be at peace for a single moment. I had started to feel like walking dead. Nothing made sense to me and not a moment of my life seemed significant to me.

I knew I could get sloshed and stoned right now, but nothing would put me at rest. If anything possibly could, it was finding Christa.

Venkat saw me next morning at the office.

"So. What have you thought?" he came and sat next to me.

"I don't know. What do we do? Visit the cops again?" I asked.

"No man. Visit them only if you know the exact procedure. I don't want another crazy encounter with them. Yesterday I had already hallucinated myself getting arrested and sodomised at the prison while we stood there at the road"

"Fuck cops! That's what you said yesterday! Remember?" I asked smirking at him.

""I did but..."

"Now shut up and live up to your words!"

"What?"

"Yes. Let's go the Hari Nagar police station. That's the closest one to Tihar I think."

"What? Not another random visit please. What do you plan to do once we get there?" he asked.

"We will figure that out."

"I don't think it's a good idea"

"It is. Let's go now."

"Now?"

"Yes."

"We can't go right now! What about the meeting?"

"I don't know. You handle the meeting. I'm going." I said and left.

I pulled over as the car approached the police station entrance.

My phone rang. It was Venkat.

"Dude. The meeting. Harry would go mad. Come soon."

"It shouldn't take very long. You handle him" I said and disconnected.

I knew missing the meeting was unreasonable. But client meetings and Harry's rebuttals had ceased to matter to me. What mattered was any faint lead that could get me the answers to the questions in my head and douse my restlessness.

I walked up to the station entrance. Few cops sitting in a jeep outside looked at me languorously.

I walked in. There was an unattended desk. I sighted a constable resting on a waiting bench at the corner.

"What do you want?" he asked me gesturing with his hand.

"I have to meet the officer. It's something important" I responded.

"What is it?" he asked yawning and sat up on the bench.

I looked at him as he growled and scratched his paunch, probably only half awake or drunk from his overnight duty.

"I can tell the officer. When will he be here?" I asked.

"He will come in sometime. You can sit there." He said signalling towards another rickety bench. "What is the case? Mobile phone theft? Pickpocket?"

"We will wait outside for the officer" I said and we came out to the porch.

The officer arrived after around half an hour of waiting.

"What is it?" he said looking at me as he hurriedly climbed up the staircase to the police station.

I went in and noticed he was busy collecting some stuff and was readying to leave the station again.

"What is it? Any report?" he asked me again busy settling his papers and files.

"I have to meet a prisoner in Tihar Jail" I said.

He suddenly looked up from what he was doing and scanned me with his eyes.

"Then go to Tihar Jail. What are you doing here?" he said after a moment and went back to his work.

"I went there already. But the cops there just won't listen!" I blurted.

He suddenly looked up and stared at me. Probably ready to blast in rage or worse still bend over and hold me by the collar.

"See. Sir. I'm very sorry. It's just that I'm in a bit of a problem. I need to meet an old friend who is serving time in Tihar Jail and I want to enquire about the process involved in this." I spoke calmly, trying to make up for my sudden utterance.

He still seemed enraged. With his frowning eyes fixed at me.

"Why do you want to go there? Is he your relative?" he asked.

"Not he. She. I want to go to the women's prison Sir."

"Women's prison?" he said and looked up at me.

"Yes" I replied.

"Don't you know? You cannot enter women's prison just like that! Either you have to be husband or close relative of the inmate. Else she has to nominate your name to the jailor. You will have to furnish identity proof against that name to be let in."

"What?" I asked in shock.

"Yes Sir!" he replied in his thumping voice.

I sat there stunned. There was no way, if Christa was inside the jail, that I could get her to nominate my name as a visitor. I knew I could bribe my way into something that was in control of this dorky policeman. Tihar seemed miles away from it. But I still decided I would give it a shot.

"What else do you want?" his loud voice shook me up.

"Sir. I really want to visit in there. It's very important." I said.

He looked at me for a moment and replied, "Then go and visit. Why are you telling me?"

"I can't get my name nominated. Neither am I any relative, Sir. I want your help in this. " I said and kept my wallet on the table. Still clenching it but trying to make the intention of bribe obvious.

He suddenly looked around to see if the constable was asleep and there wasn't anyone else around. Thankfully there wasn't. He then got up from his chair and gave me a hard, deep look. My pulse raced.

"See, whosoever you are. Tihar rules aren't child's play. It's not like a movie theatre where you get a ticket in black and enter. You cannot meet a female prisoner just like that and no bribe would work in this case. Either go get some minister or simply follow the rules. You getting it?"

I synced in his words and nodded after a moment.

"You have talked to me respectfully, and you seem worried, so take that as an advice from me" he said.

"Thank you" I replied, relived that the blatant offer for bribe didn't psyche him out.

"If you have got all the info you may leave" he said going back to his work.

I walked out of the station.

Tired and frustrated, I sat in the car and drove straightaway to Venkat's house.

There were missed calls and a text from Venkat – "Why aren't you answering? Meeting will start soon. Really need you here. I haven't even read the reports!"

I knew not being present at the meeting would create a major ruckus in office. But everything had ceased to matter to me. I knew there would soon be a call from Harry. I poured myself a drink and rolled a joint.

I switched off the lights of the room and drank and smoked up continuously for more than an hour.

It didn't give me any peace.

The more neat whisky I downed and deep drags of hash I took in, the more maddening was the commotion of thoughts in my mind.

Finding Christa seemed impossible now. And giving up on it couldn't be an option to me.

"Where the fuck are you dude!" Venkat's call woke me up after sometime.

I partially opened my eyes and tried to register his words.

He talked something about Harry and the screwed up meeting. He seemed freaked out, but it didn't bother my mind even to the extent of making an effort to move and sit up on the couch on which I lay passed out.

"Fuck Harry!" I muttered into the phone and disconnected.

I switched off the cell, tossed it aside and went back to my slumber.

✿✿

Days went by and my frustration and helplessness rose, I got back to smoking up daily and abruptly lost all the social contacts I had.

After a few days of no response from me, the party invites stopped. No one cared to know where I had disappeared.

The smoky discotheques and murky binge drinking parties continued within themselves, while I was thrown out of that world and let to perish in the one filled with haunting thoughts of Christa and helplessness which sapped my soul to the point of no return.

I started staying over at Venkat's place most of the days. Sitting through office meetings became a daunting task. In the evenings, while Venkat left for house parties or get-togethers, I locked myself up in the empty house and drank and smoked up till I passed out.

One day when there was no liquor, I decided to step out and search a local drinking spot near Venkat's house. It was past eleven and all the counters I knew were closed down. Venkat was to stay over at some far off farmhouse, and I had to spend the night alone in his house.

As a norm, I needed hash and alcohol to pass the night. I hadn't dined but food seemed secondary. I had become habitual of starving myself for no particular reason. I aimlessly kept strolling down the roads on the cold windy night, looking out for a place from where I could score any kind of hooch or grass at this time.

Most of the roads were foggy and deserted except for the traffic that hurtled by and a few men hurdled around bonfires by the roadside.

I walked up to one of the groups and asked them where I could get alcohol at this time, making the hand gesture which was the trademark gesture in Delhi to communicate your need for liquor.

One of the men guided me towards an inconspicuous street little ahead of me which was adjoining the road. I walked forward and turned into the street. It was a dark, narrow alley with thick line-up of slums lined up on both sides.

I stooped to avoid the protruding canopies and stepped ahead apprehensively.

A street kid appeared out of nowhere and stood right in front of me.

Fixing his eyes on me, he scanned me from head to toe and did the same hand gesture that I had done a few minutes ago to the man beside the bonfire – 'Liquor?'

I smiled at him for the impishness on his face and nodded.

He immediately turned around and asked me to follow him into the lane. I further stooped and walked in following the boy deeper into the rigidly packed slum network.

After a few confusing turns we were at a series of small concrete houses lining the street. The boy stopped by at one of them and knocked the door.

The door opened to blaring Hindi music and a loud, boisterous cacophony of laughter and hoots.

Before I entered, the boy stretched forward his hand for me to tip him and ran back into the slums.

The door behind me shut back as soon as I entered in. The

place looked like a small, stuffy garage with everything stacked away at a corner to transform it into a bar by the night.

Crass Hindi music blared in the overhead speakers. The lighting had been brought down to a morbid dim red, which mixed with the smoke was making the air of the room stuffy and infested with gloom.

Lungi clad men sat on stools huddled around round tables, playing rummy and drinking cheap country liquor. I noticed most of them were day-labourers, cabbies and cart pullers. They scanned me as I stood in middle of the room in my office formals looking out for a corner to sit amongst the scattered arrangement of chairs and tables.

Soon their eyes went back to their tables and I found an unoccupied stool at the counter.

Without my saying a word, the old man behind the bar pulled up a timeworn, yellowing glass and kept it in front of me with a bottle of rum. A boy walked up to me with a small platter of fried chicken sprinkled with spices and kept it next to the bottle.

I looked at other tables; they were laden with same plates, glasses and rum bottles.

I soon found myself nibbling on the chicken and sipping the country liquor, leisurely settling into the unfamiliar atmosphere around.

I looked around the bar and the boy who was frying chicken at a corner was constantly staring on me, fixing his eyes on me unaware that I was looking back at him.

I walked up to him, making sure I don't bump into a rummy-busy table.

"What happened, kid?" I asked him finding a stool to sit next to his makeshift kitchen counter.

He seemed frightened, probably expecting me to rough him up.

"I'm sorry. Did I disturb you?" he asked speaking hesitantly in rural Hindi.

I smiled at him and ruffled up his hair, "No boy, I'm already disturbed."

He smiled back at me and asked, "Why are you wearing such good clothes?"

"Just like that" I replied swigging down my drink and filling up another one.

"Do you go to an office?" he asked, with his eyes fixed on my watch.

"Yeah, only sometimes" I replied and laughed to myself.

"Did you go to school also?" he asked.

"Yeah" I murmured, hoping his questions to stop.

"Then what are you doing here?"

I looked up at his innocent face, searching for an answer in my mind.

I didn't have any.

I looked around the small, stuffy room, heavily reeking of cheap cannabis and malt. Here I am, I thought, getting drunk on street side liquor, in an unknown shanty, sitting amongst a group of rural, derelict men, and listening to b-grade Hindi and *Bhojpuri* songs.

I looked at the kid, his eyes were still fixed at me, probably seeking the answer.

I shrugged and said, "Shit happens, kid. Shit happens."

He smiled and went back to his work.

I turned back and saw one of the men sitting at a table close to me smiling at me, flashing his brassy teeth behind his thick stubble.

It struck me that the face was familiar to me. But I was tipsy, and the place was dangerous, so I chose to look away hoping he would get back to the playing cards in his hand.

"Ali *bhai.* Right?" he called out.

I immediately turned back to him. He still hadn't done away with the smile.

I returned the smile. Still trying to recall the face.

He got up from his chair and walked towards me, almost tripping over in the process.

"Ali *bhai.* How are you?" he said and shook my hand.

"Rafiq! The cab driver!" I exclaimed the moment I got a close look of his face and his same old betel stained teeth.

"Yes Ali *bhai.* Been so long but I still recognised you. Great isn't it?" He said and pulled me towards his table. "Come Ali *bhai.* Sit with us."

"No, no Rafiq. I should be leaving. It's late."

"I will drop you Ali *bhai.* Don't worry. But what are you doing here? And you've got so thin. Do you have fever? Is everything okay?" he asked.

"Yes, yes. Everything is fine." I said avoiding his questions.

"Then come and sit with us. We will make your mood much better. Come." He said pulling me towards the group of men he was sitting with.

I relented.

"Come Sir. Come. Sit here.", a man hurriedly pulled up a stool and gave me a wide smile as I reached the table.

The table was heavily stacked with empty bottles of rum, packs of beedis and empty chicken platters. Rafiq got a new glass and poured me more rum.

One of them ordered new chicken platters for us. I looked around at the group of men, some of them had quietly fixed their eyes on me, probably wondering how I had landed up in that run down bar.

"Ali *bhai,* this is rum, and this is rummy. "Rafiq announced towards me raising both his arms with a glass in one hand and a pack of cards in the other, "Welcome to our world!" he said and everybody laughed hoarsely.

I soon started playing cards with the men and my glass kept refilling several times on insistence from someone or the other from the group.

When I decided to leave, paying the combined bill for the table, Rafiq was to drop me till Venkat's apartment which wasn't very far and as we got up he started introducing me to each of the men in the big group.

Almost all of them were drivers like him. Too inebriated to take notice, I smiled at and shook hands with each of them, barely registering any of the names Rafiq spoke.

There was one fellow who had been unusually quiet and discreet throughout my time at the table. He had barely looked up from his glass and whenever I glanced at him he was just downing more and more liquor. He seemed sad, distressed, and indifferent to any of what was going on at the table.

Noticing he was the only one who was still sitting, Rafiq patted his back and said, "C'mon Rajesh. It will be fine. Don't take so much tension. Everything will be okay."

Few other men also patted his back and said similar words like Rafiq.

I was too tipsy to get into any conversation, but since I was standing in the middle of the group while this was happening, I had to ask Rafiq out of courtesy, "What happened to him?"

"He is very depressed Ali bhai. He married recently. His wife worked as a domestic help and got picked up by police on theft charges. They locked her up in Tihar and they're asking a big bribe now! Assholes, I tell you. Look at the poor fellow." he said wincing at the guy.

I stared at him as Rafiq's word slowly registered in my head.

I looked at Rafiq, "Really?" I asked.

"Yes Ali bhai. That's why he is so depressed." he said.

I looked at Rafiq in stunned silence.

"Did you just say Tihar jail?" I asked after a moment.

"Yes Ali bhai. They locked her up in Tihar. But what happened to you? Why are you so shocked?" he asked waving at my expressionless face staring at him.

"You gotta help me out Rafiq!" I blurted.

"Help? Sure Ali *bhai*. What happened?" he asked.

I let out a heavy sigh and replied, "Rafiq, you were right. I'm not okay. I have lost weight. I've become an alcoholic. I also do drugs. And now, it's only you who can help me."

He looked at me with a confused face and asked, "Me?"

"Sir, you sure they would let you in?" Rajesh asked as we waited for our turn in the serpentine queue outside Tihar Jail main entrance.

Rajesh was a young fellow in his twenties. When last night I accidentally heard his story from Rafiq, I knew right away that I had landed up in that bar for a reason. I pleaded Rajesh to visit his wife in Tihar the very next morning and to tag me along.

Rajesh had been harassed by the police for a petty case of jewellery theft for which his wife was picked on and locked.

The queue of around three hundred people, all of whom were registered visitors to Tihar, looked like a regular drill for him.

He looked like a tired, timid man who was thrown into the ruthless red-tapism of the police. Rafiq told me he had married just three months ago, when their ends didn't meet through his job as a cart-puller, his wife opted to work as a maid in the apartments near the slums.

"She hadn't stolen anything s*aab*." he said to me, with the frustration and resign that seemed familiar on his face by now, "It's been a month already since she's inside. And the police doesn't even listen to me. All they say is pay up or they won't leave her for a very long time!"

"Don't worry. She'll soon be out." that was all I could reply with. I knew that I hardly cared for the rigid set of problems Rajesh was in. As we slowly approached the huge iron gates of Tihar, all I could think about was getting past the cops posted there. In a corner of my mind, I wondered if I was heading towards Christa with my every step forward in that queue, or atleast will the next few hours bring me the peace I had been longing for since more than an year.

My heart pounded harder as we got closer to the entrance with just few people in front of us in the queue.

There were two cops manning the big gates.

"Just be confident and do as we said" Rafiq told Rajesh, "When the cops ask, tell them his name is Mahesh. He is Laxmi's brother. Talk to them confidently. Okay?"

Rajesh nodded hesitantly.

"Idiot why are you so scared?" Rafiq asked patting Rajesh behind his head, "What will those motherfuckers do? Will they eat you up? Talk to them confidently okay. We will soon get your wife out. For now Ali *bhai* really need your help. You gotta be smart and help him. Okay?"

Rajesh continued nodding.

Rafiq drifted aside when we had almost gotten at the entrance.

The cops checked the ID and entry-pass of the couple of men in front of me and let them in.

Rajesh's turn came. I stood behind him and for a moment looked up at the gigantic entry gates overshadowing both of us.

"Central Jail No. 4, Tihar" the semi-circular board displayed in flaking paint.

"Who's Mahesh?" one of the cops said looking at Rajesh's entry form.

"He is Mahesh, *saab*. My wife's brother. He also wants to meet her." Rajesh answered timidly.

The cop looked at me, scanning me from top to bottom.

My heart thumped. I could see the dark hallway behind the partially open gates. The view fired up my deep gutted desperation to get inside and seek all my answers.

"Okay. Go. But from next time you also register yourself" the cop's announced towards me.

"Okay Sir. Definitely. Thank you!" I said and we rushed forward.

The guards opened the small door affixed in the gate.

We stooped in our way into the dark hallway.

"Finally!" I sighed to myself, "Thanks Rajesh. I owe you one." I said and hugged Rajesh.

"No problem *saab*." he replied softly with the refinement in his voice.

As I looked at the high walls of the long, dimly lit corridor. Rajesh seemed familiar with the place.

I followed him as he strode forward into the corridor.

The corridor got pitch dark as we walked deeper into the hallway.

The foul smell and stuffiness in the air got stronger.

I looked around. There was absolutely no ventilation. In the darkness I could see the greying and peeling off walls. It was unsettling.

"Where are we heading, Rajesh" I asked seeing Rajesh's dark figure walking little ahead of me.

"Come, *saab.* We're almost there." He replied.

Rajesh seemed aloof the moment we had gained access into the prison courtyard. He probably knew that Rafiq and I have talked him into being used as a token to fulfil my need. He knew the person he was helping hardly cared for what he was going through.

And now, feeling the gloom and stodge filling the place and the fact that his newly wed wife was locked up in here, I felt for him for the first time.

The courtyard led us to another set of entry gates, similar to the main entrance, through which visitors were being passed after thorough frisking.

We joined the small queue at the gate. The frisking consisted of metal detection and body scanners. Cellphones, car keys, cigarette packets and even pens were to be handed over at the entrance before entering.

Our entry-form was stamped with the text "Admit two - 1 hour permit"

We again stooped through the small door affixed in the gates opening into the meeting hall.

Suddenly, a disturbing melee of people and voices baffled me. I looked around the gigantic hall, plastic chairs laid strewn across randomly. The stuffy, unventilated room was choked up with more than three hundred people waiting to meet the prisoners. Some of them brawled and argued. Loud wails of infant children waiting to meet their prisoner mothers echoed through the hall.

I noticed Rajesh's eyes getting red and heavy.

"There is no order here, *saab.* We will have to keep watching those windows" he said pointing towards a series of windows shielded with iron grills, "When Laxmi comes there, we will go."

I nodded. Rajesh was on the verge of breaking down. I looked away, pretending I hadn't noticed his teary eyes. I knew my keeping a hand on his shoulder and consoling him will not get his wife on this side of those grills. And worse, he knew I was indifferent.

We passed time finding a corner to sit on the bare floor. I kept my eyes fixed on the queue of windows. Every batch of meetings lasted for more than an hour. The visitors at the window, touched, held and kissed the prisoners inside through the grills. Some of them cried too loudly and were shouted at by the women guards.

"You can take a nap, *saab.* It will take atleast four - five hours." Rajesh said seeing me restlessly watching every activity at the windows.

We passed the hours by trying to rest our head on the wall behind us and taking small naps. Trying to sleep seemed a much better option than keeping your eyes and ears open in that hall and watching each and every morbid face repeatedly.

"Rajesh Kumar" a female guard's voice resonated through the hall.

Rajesh hurriedly got up and rushed towards the windows raising his one hand up. I followed him.

The guard checked our form and scribbled the time on it.

"Window 9" she said and guided us towards the last window in the queue.

We walked through the queue of crowded windows to reach the one where Rajesh's wife sat on the other side.

Rajesh rushed forward as the window approached and grabbed Laxmi's hands jutting out through the grills.

Both of them began to sob.

Rajesh spoke something in rural Hindi, words which sounded like he had talked to a local lawyer in the slums and he had guaranteed that she will be out.

Standing behind Rajesh, looking at him sobbing softly and holding his wife's hand, talking about the food in the jail and calculating each hundred rupee that he had planned to save and borrow to get her out, tears surfaced my eyes and my throat began to choke up.

The state of distress and adversity around me gave me a jolt of reality about what hardship and frustration can really mean. When a toddler gets to see his mother only once a month, through those rusty grills and amid that stuffy stench of sweat and bile, a young adult like me griping over a lost love over a glass of whiskey or by getting drunk and hooked in a rave party ceased to exist in that room.

"Who is he?" Laxmi's voice cut through my thoughts.

I looked at her. She looked like a young girl in her late teens. The jail seemed to have hardened her, which reflected in her teary but composed eyes. Beneath that layer of composure was the playfulness and innocence of a teenaged girl, which I wished the jail would never take away from her.

"Oh yes. I forgot. This is a *saab* from the city, Laxmi. He says he needs little help from you." Rajesh said and got up from his stool, asking me to sit.

"Laxmi, my name is Ali. I'm your husband's friend's friend." I said, struggling to find the right words to speak to her.

"Talk to *saab* properly. Listen to him." Rajesh said seeing her getting pensive.

"Laxmi, we will soon bail you out of this place. We sure will. Okay?" I said trying to make my words sound consoling towards her.

She just looked down and nodded. Probably having her ears tired from listening to that.

"Laxmi, I'm sorry to disturb you. I really am. But I need little information from your prison and you can easily help me in that." I said trying to break it down into as much rural Hindi as I knew.

"From here? The prison?" She asked and looked at Rajesh apprehensively. He nodded at her with an expression of assurance, "Talk to *saab,* Laxmi. He is a good man. He just needs some information." he said.

"Okay" she looking at me, waiting for me to start speaking.

"Laxmi, do you know all the women in this prison?" I asked.

She thought for a moment and said, "I think so *saab.* I have been here for a month now. I think I know most of them atleast by their names"

"By names is enough. I'm looking for a woman and I want to know if she is here in this prison. She's not an Indian. She's a white, a foreigner." I said speaking in slow and clear Hindi and giving her time to think.

"What's her name? There are many *gori* women in here, *saab*" she said.

"Christa Mathews. That's the name. Think and tell me Laxmi, do you any woman by the name Christa? Have you heard this name anywhere in the prison?" I asked.

"Christa?" she repeated the name to herself, straining her memory and mulling over it. My pulse raced as I looked at her closely in anticipation of her answer.

"No" she suddenly blurted.

"No? What no?" I asked.

"There's no *gori* by the name Christa, *saab.*" she said looking at me.

"Are you sure Laxmi?" I asked trying to make her think harder.

"Yes, *saab.* I've been around for a month and I have never heard that name. I've even mingled with the *goris* many times." she said, with a part of her mind still mulling over the name.

I looked back at Rajesh. He gave me a wide smile, "Are you relived now, *saab*?" he asked.

'Is this it?' I thought to myself. I looked at the smiling faces of Rajesh and Laxmi, they didn't know who I was looking for or what my problem was. But they knew it was always a good news if you're looking for a person and you don't find them in the jail.

I smiled back at them. It was like a shot of life into my walking-dead body. In a bout of elation, I got up and hugged Rajesh tightly.

"Thanks. My friend, thanks. You've no idea how much you've helped me" I said respiring of relief.

"I didn't do anything, s*aab.* I'm happy for you" he said looking at the watch. The gloom in his eyes had returned. The one hour meeting permit was coming to an end.

He moved away from me and looked at the window. There was no one. The chair on the other side was empty.

"Where's Laxmi?" I asked puzzled.

"She must have gone to her cell, *saab.* She knits sweaters for me. She must have gone to get it." he said and sat on the chair.

"Wow. She's a beautiful and intelligent woman, Rajesh. And she really loves you. You must be happy. Don't worry; she will soon walk out free. Just be patient." I said the customary words, which sure sounded corny, and stepped backwards to wait for him.

I turned my back towards the window, to let them have the privacy of comfortably seeing each other off once Laxmi would return.

"*Saab*" Laxmi's voice called me out from behind.

I turned around to see a newly knit sweater in Rajesh's hand. He was smiling.

"What happened, Laxmi?" I asked walking up to the window.

"She is Lalli. A *gori* friend of mine. I got her along with me in case you want to ask her anything. She knows all the *goris* in here very well. And she understands English too." Laxmi said pointing at a woman standing next to her.

"No it's okay really" I smiled and turned towards the women. She was smiling back.

I looked at her closely through the dim light and rusty bars. I began to ask something but stopped. She looked like a hardened prison junkie - Crew-cut hair, heavily tanned skin, and baggy, cold eyes. But there was something unnerving about her. I stooped closer towards the window and looked at the face closely.

The smile on her face disappeared.

She was Christa.

Goosebumps ran down my body. Suddenly there was no noise, no people, no thoughts; I just stared at her hardy recognizable face vacantly.

"Ali" she whispered looking at me dazed.

I tried to come up with words but choked up.

She leapt forward and clenched the bars.

"Ali" she shouted in my face. Her loud cry suddenly brought my frozen body to life.

A woman prison-guard pulled her away from the window, shouting at her and trying to drag her back into the prison.

She resisted and ran back towards me.

"What's going on here?" an officer held me by my arm and pulled me back.

"Christa!" I shouted towards her. "Leave me. Leave me you motherfucker!" I got hysterical and violently jerked the officer off my body.

He lost balance and hit his head on the floor with a thud.

Three constables charged towards me. One of them plunged the butt of his rifle into my stomach as I ran to the window.

I doubled up and collapsed on the floor.

"Ali!" I heard Christa's cry from behind the window.

I struggled to stand back but the injured officer walked up to me and gave me another hard kick in my stomach.

I spewed blood and bile and again collapsed on the floor.

Loud cries of Crista resonated through the hall. Through my giddy vision I could see the officer again walking towards me, Rajesh tried to hold him back by falling to his feet. He pushed him aside and gave me another hard blow in my gut.

I blacked out.

13

CHRISTA SPEAKS PART 2

Sometimes, I sit myself down and try to think straight about my life. It's never as easy as it sounds, but then I try. Cos' I have the time, all of it, gnawing into me each moment of the day. So all I do is think, and think more.

I was 25, freshly broken up with my boyfriend, having a job that paid me peanuts, and a life that I hated.

When I was content that it can't get worse, I was put on a plane to India.

My wallet had 300 euros, my backpack had none. The amount was expected to last me a couple of months, or the time I take to do the job I was given.

Through all the noise, chaos, smell, sweat and grime, I realised that if it's anything that makes India liveable, it's the Indians.

India was a maze and I soon started fitting into the maze

that I once found confounding. Days passed by and I stopped counting the number of days I had already spent here or the number of days I further had to.

When I had almost convinced myself that relocating cities and visiting prisons was the only purpose of my existence, I met Ali - a tall, gauntly looking young Indian male in his twenties. My first impression if him was of a just another dope head, lost in his own world and seemingly content with life. A look into his eyes later in time revealed to me what a quiet conflict deep within a soul could mean. I could relate to him.

Within three months of being in India, my diplomat visa expiration and my call to return was summoned to me by the embassy. The summon letter said I had done a good job, it said I withstood unfavourable locales and had delivered what I was supposed to – the whereabouts of the twelve Italian tourists. But what it didn't mention was beneath that supposed good job, I had done a terrible job. That of falling in love while at work. In love with India. And in love with Ali.

The email elegantly attached with a letter asking me to be done and dusted with India and return back to my home country while I was still in my legal diplomat status snapped me out my demonic self-denial mode. I wanted to believe that I had been waiting for this letter every moment since last three months, but reality told me I wasn't. I wanted to believe that it was easy to leave Ali behind, but I couldn't.

The more I tried to convince myself that finding love in India and Ali was insane and going back as per plan was what I needed to do, the more I could convince myself to take it the other way round. May be it was the strange desolation that I dreaded, but I decided to stay on.

People say when you connect back the dots of your life,

there are a few moments which you still find staring back at you in the face. You imagine how it'd have been if you had a chance to go on without connecting them. As I write this, I see that moment right now, staring back at me relentlessly, not ready to give up. When I think of an alternative path which could have transpired had I not connected it, I see a helpless, disturbing void space. So I connect it and move on.

Willing and reluctant at the same time, I soon started a hurried process of finding a means to stay on in India. It was a race against time, as I had my diplomat status expiring within a month. I was severely cash strapped too, I had 3 grands of Indian currency with me, and last months' housing bills were still to be paid.

The embassy helpline phoned me and asked me to notify the preferred dates for my departure back to Italy, I was also told that I will not be able to reimburse any expenses post the date of the call. In short, while I was clearly instructed to leave India, I was desperately figuring out some way to stay back here.

Absconding from the job and melting into the ubiquitous hippie crowd at Paharganj wasn't an option to me, I was on a diplomat Visa, a fact that ensured I shall and will be traced back where ever I am.

Days went by. My closeness with Ali and the desperation to find a way to stay back grew manifold, always ticking like clockwork in my mind.

And then it all boiled down to one single day, when I was penniless and clueless about where I was headed to. I sat in my room, clutching my head with both my hands and trying to figure out what can stop me from finding myself aboard a flight to Italy within next three days.

I had multiple reminders from the embassy in form of emails and calls. I had run out of cash. And with the final deadline of my stay just a week away, I still had no plan to evade the expected.

It was then when I got a call from Fred. When I look back and connect the dots, I see this as one of those moments, haunting me with a constant stare from the paper of my journal.

Fred was a fellow foreigner I had met in Delhi who lived by peddling and bootlegging everything that Indian Government deems illegal. His fortnightly catch up calls, which had seemed pestering till the moment seemed like a vent out right now. It was the first time I told anyone what I was into and what I needed. Expecting consolation and not a solution, I waited for his answer from the other side of the phone.

"It's simple, no big deal. I can help you out", pat same the reply.

I listened to him astounded and dazed as he dictated to me the downfall of a life that I was about to get into.

Fred told me I could get a new tourist visa as soon as my existing visa expires. It was impossible but a hundred thousand in cold cash would make it possible. If I wanted to stay back I was to get him the money within a day's time. Fact was that I was completely broke. Fred had a solution for that too. Smuggling small consignments of cocaine out of India was one of Fred's jobs. He asked me to do it for him and make a quick buck out of it. The money would go into shady back office payments to process my application faster and effectively, and to evade the background check for the new visa, something which would reveal my existing visa status.

After Fred had completed talking, I had only one thing to say, "I'll do it".

Within an hours' time, I found myself packing up my stuff to travel to Pondicherry, which was the nearest seaport from Bangalore, as soon as possible.

I had no money, so I had to force Ali to drive me there. Ali didn't know about what I was upto, so I had to make it look like a leisure trip.

Within few hours, we were at a secluded beach in Pondicherry. Ann had travelled along with me as I couldn't site a valid enough reason when she insisted upon tagging along.

The moment I spotted Fred from a distance at the beach, I knew what the big trolley bag next to him was stuffed with. He had travelled from Delhi to Pondicherry, which was almost halfway down the country, on a days' notice. He was to return the same or next day, and going by the size of the bag with him it looked like he was to stay for a month.

When I had later asked him about chances of getting caught at the port while smuggling out a suitcase full of pristine cocaine, he had fallen silent and looked at me for blankly for a while, soon, he responded with an unconvincing negative.

By midnight, we were at the port. Ali and Ann were in deep sleep at the cottage.

The port was completely deserted except few ships anchored at a far off distance. With the mix of grey sea waves hitting the shore and a heavily clouded, deep black sky, the place looked almost ghostly in the night.

I looked at Fred in the dark and he flashed a wide, almost unsettling smile which made him look like a part of the setting.

Before I could say anything, he passed me the handle of the bag and said, "Christa, don't be afraid. Just be cool. This place is totally safe even for a murder."

He said it with a menacing ease and contentment, I was suddenly sure that the man in front of me had killed men with his bare hands. He also must have raped and killed women. With a chill running down my spine, I smiled back at him.

I looked at the bag and tried to divert my mind into what I was supposed to do. I was to walk up to the shore when a boat would arrive and handover the bag to the men manning the boat. Fred was to go and wait at the street away from the shore, as the men in the boat would go back if they see more than one person present when they approach the port.

Fred left me with the bag and disappeared in the dark. I stood frozen in the whistling wind with loud sea waves dying out just before my feet, as if trying to warn me about some danger but falling just short every time.

I soon spotted a bright flash light slowly approaching me from the sea. I tried to pull the heavily loaded bag as its wheels immersed deep into the sand. Profusely palpitating and having my own heartbeat ringing inside me louder than anything around, I pulled the cocaine suitcase forward and started walking towards the shore.

The flashlight came closer and I could figure out a motor boat with two men looking straight at me. One of them flashed a wide smile which I tried to return.

He jumped out of the motorboat and briskly walked towards me with the flashlight.

'Sixty two sixty' he said when he had almost walked upto me. 'Thirty nine eighty' I responded with a shaking voice. These were the code numbers we both were expecting from each other. I was told that if I hear a different number, I was to politely apologise and say that I'm not carrying what he was expecting me to, either in quantity or in quality. If he hears a different number, he will back off with a similar apology and go back to his boat immediately. 'There will not be any physical contact, not even an accidental brushoff of hands, until total deal is completed' Fred had told me.

A total deal meant that this man, after the numbers were matched, was to squat down where he was standing and put down the bag in front of him. He will then open the zippers of the bag from all sides and check the quantity of the consignment to his satisfaction. After that would be the quality check, in which he would either taste a pinch of the powder or use a test-tube with a liquid to check how quick the solution turns blue. If the check is unsuccessful in any means, he will ask me to take back my stuff and turn back and leave once he ensures that I have placed my hand back on the bag. If the check goes successful, he will call the other person from the boat to bring in the bag of cash and I will be given the bag.

The person in front of me did all of it. Without saying a word, he squatted down in front of me, zipped open the bag and checked the quantity. It was the first time I saw what I was carrying. The bag was filled till the last ounce it could accommodate. The plastic bags filled with the powder were randomly stuffed in the bag and duct taped together. After the quantity drill he slit open one of the packets and placed the pinch of the stuff on his tongue. Without going for the test tube check, he zipped back the bag and got up from the sitting position. He then turned back to the man in the boat and signalled him to come.

I let out a heavy sigh of relief, and waited for the other man to give me the bag so that I run out towards the street with a million rupees, of which I would get a tenth.

The other man strode towards me steadfastly, as if he'd been waiting for the signal. I noticed he had nothing in his hands, and as far as I knew, one couldn't stuff a million Indian rupees in their pockets.

As soon as he reached me, he fished out a hand cuff out of nowhere and locked up my hands. Before I could react or unfreeze myself, he had the keys in his pockets and his *'Puducherry Police'* ID card thrust right into my face.

He started walking me towards the Police Jeep which had pulled over at a distance from the beach. I was made to climb into the stuffy and dark canopy. A female constable looked at me with a grumpy face and shouted something at me. Her voice drowned out into the shock and numbness in my mind. I had one last look at the beach through the meshed window, which was probably my last sight of freedom. The jeep ignited and dragged itself into darkness, taking me into a territory unknown.

"On December 10th 2010, a foreigner woman was caught red handed at a Pondicherry beach trafficking 19 kilos of Grade A cocaine late in the night." The local papers flashed the next day.

Some said she was an established trafficker. Some said she was a hippie trying to make a quick buck. Some even said she was a hooker. The news faded into the pages and gradually disappeared.

The Pondicherry Police, observing my Italian passport, didn't know what to do of me. So I, along with the cocaine, was dumped in a goods carrier train.

After lying lifelessly for two days in the squalid bogie which reeked of urine, cattle and horse-shit, and after losing the sense of time, the iron gates of the bogie opened at the New Delhi Railway Station. Few policemen escorted me to a long walk towards a jeep waiting for me.

I looked around, drowned out and almost dead, and tried to absorb the fact that I was transported to the capital city of India – ironically back to the place where I had first landed more than a year back.

The station should have felt very familiar to me, but when you're dragged out of a dark dungeon from an almost lifeless state with your hands chained and suddenly a dozen khaki clad men start shepherding you, the world looks different.

My hands were finally released when the handcuffs over my ulcerated wrists were unlocked in exchange of bigger, more demonic shackles. One which didn't lock my hands but gnawed right into my soul – The Tihar Jail.

Today, two years down the line and after going thru phases of questioning my own sanity, I have accepted the fact that I belong here. I was set up by Fred, as the inmates told later me. I was the deal Fred had struck with the police to buy out his release from this very same prison. The police wanted a weighty cocaine catch and a man to fill up the prison. I was served on a platter.

Fred had once told me that nothing comes free, and when it does, you should doubt it. So I don't blame him for what he did. I should have doubted him.

I think the jail has tranquilized me now. A few months into this place made me discard my emotions down the drain.

When I walked to the meeting room the day you had come to meet me, I wasn't as shocked as I thought I should have been. Cos' somewhere in my mind, in the faintest, darkest corner I refused to visit, I always had this firm belief that someday I'll definitely find you standing on the other side of these rusted iron grills, looking for me.

And now, as I complete this letter, I have a feeling in my heart that it was all somehow worth it – the meeting, the love, the jail, and finally the place called India.

Someday, away from all this, I hope to spend a day with you, and hope I give you a complete story which you'd asked from me.

Christa Matthews.
Ward no. 14, Tihar Jail.

EPILOGUE:

Someone bangs the door of the restroom. I suddenly realise it's been more than long since I have been sitting here. I fold back the letter and try to tuck it back in my wallet. I notice it's quite worn out now, almost giving way at the creases.

The bang happens again, "Who's in there? You passed out?" someone yells.

"Yeah, coming" I shout back.

I get up and splash the freezing tap water repeatedly on my face, almost burning the insides of my eyes.

I look in the yellowing mirror. I stare hard, and look into my own eyes thru the texture of scratches. "Get yourself together" I whisper to myself, but the red, bloodshot eyes I am looking into have a different story to say - one of regrets and solace, of cold comfort and hard reality, of love and despair, and of fragile happiness and lasting helplessness.

The mirror takes me to the dingy garage cum bar in the

slum area of Delhi, there's Rafiq sitting at the corner with his loud group. The same kid at the corner is frying chicken and serving it in the same platter. Smell of country liquor and cheap marijuana rise thru my nostrils and makes the room stuffy. Rafiq smiles at me and signals me to join his table. Just as I step forward and move, everything disappears.

I find myself in front of a computer, there's some nagging report I'm working on and I hate how everyone around me is going frenzied about a client visit which is soon impending. Someone calls out my name from the other side; I look out and see it's my boss Mike. He is signalling me to go with him for a coffee break. I could really use some caffeine and a smoke right now, so I spring up from my chair, almost elated, but then suddenly Mike's gone, and so is everything around me.

There's loud peppy music around me and I'm huffing, almost panting for breath. I notice there's a treadmill under me and it's making me run. I look to my side and there's Sandy running next to me on another one. He waves at me to stop the machine and come to the juice bar for a protein shake. I'm relieved at this. I quickly press the stop button and dismount the machine. As I approach him standing at the corner, he smiles at me and asks me to walk faster. I try to sprint up but them I'm suddenly alone and in middle of nowhere. I look around, there's no gym or Sandy. Just a void filled with nothing.

I'm sitting in my room, there's Jimi Hendrix donning the wall and playing on my old stereo. The lights are dim and there are two people sitting around me in a huddle. They're talking casually and laughing; one of them pats me on the back and says, 'Ali *bhai*'. He's Raja, I realise, and next to him is Balu. I can feel we're quite high. I laugh back and ask them to pass me the hash pipe. Balu picks it up and lights it, just when I stretch my hand towards him, he's evaporates with the smoke.

I'm leisurely walking down a tree shaded avenue. The weather is pleasant, and the trees around are chiming and giving me a calm that I feel I have been lacking my entire life. Someone clasps my arm and rest their head on my shoulder, matching their steps with mine. It seems familiar. I look to my side and it's Divya. Her black, welled eyes make me see what happiness and tranquillity looks like. Suddenly I have no complains or regrets for all that I have lost on my long way. I feel the inherent rust which had sapped my soul disappearing, and giving way for long forgotten peace and blissfulness. I look at her and thank her for coming by, I tell her I was withered from within and there was no remedy I had for it except her. She smiles back; it's a little eerie, discomforting smile. Before I decipher it more, I'm all alone on that avenue. The trees are dried up and the hot sun is just above my head.

The heat of the sun transforms into a hot, stuffy room. The smells around me aren't very pleasing, and the loud wails make them further worse to stand. I somehow find the place familiar, and soon realise I'm in the Tihar Women Prison and this is the meeting lobby. The man next to me is Rajesh, who's talking to a woman standing behind the window fitted with thick and rusty iron bars. The other side of the window is dark and the iron bars make her barely visible. I can see that they're weeping, trying to hold hands thru the bars. The sight of sheer powerlessness a person can go through makes me weary and sick in my mind, and I turn to the other side and avoid letting it seep further into me. Just as I'm waiting to soon get out of the place, a voice calls me out from behind. I turn back towards the window and see it's from a woman on the other side. But she's not Rajesh's wife. I move forward and try to take a close look at her. Her vacant stare at me is discomforting. I realise she is Christa. I clasp the iron bars in disbelief. She smiles at me and asks me to go away. I feel the same powerlessness that made me sick and weary a few minutes ago now climbing over me. I ask her to come forward and talk to me, but the darkness behind the bars becomes pitch black and engulfs her into it.

"Christa!" I call out in the darkness, but the bars transform into the yellowing and scratchy mirror, and the prison waiting hall becomes the restroom.

With sweaty face and palms, I feel a chill talking over me as I look hard at myself into the mirror. I splash more tap water, which is almost freezing and again burns my eyes.

"Get yourself together Ali" I again whisper to myself and try to stop the familiar restlessness take over me.

A hard knock on the door shakes me up, the guy outside yells at me to open the door or he will break in.

I wipe the water and sweat off my face and palms and open the door. The guy outside pushes me aside and locks back the restroom door behind me.

I'm back into the loud music and the smoke filled party room.

Venkat comes to me and pats my shoulder hard, "Where were you my friend?" he asks me drunk, almost tipping over.

I don't answer and walk past him.

"I got some *Manali* hash my friend, go smoke it. Don't miss out on it." He says pointing towards a corner of the room which has gleaming black hash balls kept in a crumbled paper.

I know I can walk up to it and roll myself a joint. It will temporarily give me a high and some much needed peace. I can also land up in my bed with one of the girls from this party; all I need to do is strike a conversation and fake being loaded with money.

I go to the kitchen and make myself a coffee instead. With the mug in my hand, I walk straight to the balcony outside the house, avoiding groups of people calling out to me.

The balcony is relatively quiet with just a faint drone of the music. The icy breeze goes thru my hair and gives me a strange calm, making me forget the chill of the weather.

I sip the hot coffee and the warmth is comforting. The infinitely lit city and the foggy, starless night sky meet at a far off distance. I look blankly into it and want it to absorb me into itself. I notice my eyes welling up. Either it's the cold weather outside or the coldness that has gnawed me from within that's causing it.

My vision is going blurry. A million thoughts suddenly flood my mind. There are faces flashing and voices talking to me. Some are pleasant, while some makes me want to shut my ears and double up on the ground.

I keep wandering in the flood of people, places and voices. I see myself in times of real happiness and real friends, but I'm not welcomed there anymore. I see myself in times of love, lust and sometimes on that thin line in between. The place is abandoned and now there's nothing. At last I just see a cloud of drugs, rave parties and one night stands take over my life, it's dark and consuming. I initially try to struggle my way out but soon give in to it. It's a scary, unknown territory; it never calms you down or comforts you, it just continuously bogs you down into it making it weigh heavier over you with every passing day.

I think about Christa, the distance she went in loving me and the path I chose for myself thinking she'd left me. I remember her face behind the rusty iron grills and doubt if I'd ever be able to forget it.

I still sometimes find myself standing in the long queue outside Tihar Women's Prison on the meeting day.

'Someday, away from all this, I hope to spend a day with you', that is all I'm able to say on seeing her on the other side of the window.

Someone calls me out from the party and breaks my chain of thoughts. It's Venkat, he's getting the car for us to leave.

Walking towards the staircase, I wipe off the tears from my eyes and gulp down the remaining coffee, preparing myself to go thru another night of dreamless, dead sleep. And hoping to have a better morning tomorrow.

- Love Power Politics!!
- Love a Rather Bad Idea
- Love & Urban Melodrama
- LUV is a Dirty Business
- My Love Never Faked...
- Nothing for you my Dear
- Nothing Lasts Forever
- Of Tattoos and Taboos!
- Oops! 'I' fell in Love!
- Ouch! that 'Hearts'..
- Patyala Down De Throat
- Plz.. Kiss me or Kill me
- Reality Bytés 'Bites'
- She is Single I'm Taken
- Simple Things Make LUV
- Something in your Eyes
- Sumthing of a Mocktale
- 34 Bubblegums and Candies
- That Kiss in the Rain..
- The Dev-D Syndrome...
- The Equation of my Love
- The Funda of Mix-ology
- The Idiot-Dudes.....
- The India I Dream of
- The Journey of Rock...
- The Journey to Nowhere
- The Lost Scraps of Love
- The Off-Site Tamasha
- The Other way Round
- The Quest for Nothing!
- The Thing Between U & Me
- Those Small Lil Things
- Three Times Loser....
- To Whom it May Concern:
- When Life Tricked me..
- What... if not I.I.T.?
- Will you Marry Me Cupid

- Brain Building for achievement
  Herbert N. Casson
- Cheiro's : Language of the Hand
- Winning Personality:
  The Magic key to success
  F. Oss